THE DEVIL ATOP CAULDRON PEAK
An Epic Rocky Mountain Duel

Stephen G. Kirk

THE DEVIL ATOP CAULDRON PEAK

Stephen G. Kirk

© 2023

For Dad and Mom

For Troubles caused

Heartache Endured

Your Unending Patience & Love

A Poor Harvest

September 19th in the year of our Lord 1891, late afternoon, and the autumn sun is already casting long, elongated shadows upon the arid parched earth. George Dunn and his wife Grace stand together taking stock of this year's disappointing crop of barley and dry peas. Spring and early summer had held the promise of a good crop, but with the arrival of mid-July, the rain became infrequent before ceasing all together. The drought continued unabated throughout August and into September. The growing season is short in this part of the country, even if rains came tomorrow, it would do little but interrupt the harvest of whatever crops remained standing in the sun-baked straw brown fields.

George Dunn a Scottish settler had met his wife Grace five years before in Fort Macleod, Alberta. Then a young girl, Grace arrived there with her Métis family having fled the troubles of the 1885 North West Métis Rebellion far to the east. Though six years his wife's senior, George was little more than a youth at nineteen, while Grace had only turned fifteen several days prior to their betrothal. Despite her tender years, believing George to be as good a choice as any found in the vicinity, her father and mother gave their blessing to the union. Such marriages were anything, but uncommon in those hard years. Unlike the adolescents of future decades, both George and Grace were both capable and willing to assume their roles as adults. Life on the frontier was hard for a single man and nearly impossible for a single woman. In order to survive, each needed someone they could depend upon. They discovered what was required of a mate and partner, and within a short time, found a welcome and unexpected benefit; love.

Grace Dunn watched her husband walk into the field a short ways. Bending low, he scooped up a handful of the parched soil letting it slowly run through his fingers. Rising to his feet, George brushed back a shock of ginger hair from his eyes, stroking his beard while gazing toward the horizon. She tried to guess his thoughts and the depths of his concerns while hoping that she might help shoulder some of his burdens.

Already the sun had dropped beneath the higher peaks of the mountain range off to the west casting the lands to the east in varying shades of light and shadow. Silhouetted against the backdrop of a bright western sky, Grace thought her husband a fine figure of a man. At twenty-five years of age, the arduous labours of ranching, farming, and carving out a homestead in the harsh southern territories had forged an iron hard body and an inner resolve that would sustain them, despite the inevitable hardships that waited.

The couple's small mixed farm covered a quarter section, one hundred and sixty acres of decent bottomland bordering the eastern banks of a small tree lined creek the Sioux and Blackfoot called the Little Spitzee. Growing barley, dry peas, and some corn, they also raised a small flock of sheep, half a dozen cattle, and several horses.

The one room log home, modest barn, and its small corral sat several miles east of the North-West Mounted Police post in the settlement of Pincher Creek. The hamlet received its name when a member of the N.W.M.P. came across a pair of rusting pincers lying along a shallow creek bank; the tool lost by a group of prospectors four years earlier. Such valuable items weren't often misplaced and as the unusual discovery circulated among the locals, the Spitzee instead became known as Pincher Creek.

When the local moniker appeared in print within an 1880 Geological Survey Report, the name stuck and became official.

A decade earlier, George had left Scotland with his cousin Finn. The pair intended to start a cattle ranch in the territories having heard rumors of wealthy European financiers who knowing little or nothing of the cattle industry, had established successful ranches along the Eastern Slopes of the Rocky Mountains, in the future province of Alberta. Leasing vast tracts of land from the government for next to nothing, these investors had become nothing short of "cattle barons." George and Finn, figuring if others could manage it, they could as well. Six months after leaving Glasgow the pair had arrived in the small settlement known as Fort MacLeod. Together they found work on one of the larger ranches in the area, thinking the best way to learn a business was from the ground up. The work was hard and the pay was poor, but the boys already familiar with life's difficulties quickly learned what it meant to become a "cowboy."

The young cousins had nearly saved enough for a small spread of their own, when tragedy struck.

February, still late winter, and a Chinook wind blew eastward between the mountains passes bringing with it an unseasonable though welcome respite courtesy of Canada's west coast that lay some six hundred miles to the west. Over the space of the last several days, the wind sculpted snow drifts thinned and in some cases had vanished completely.

The ranch's cow boss had sent Finn and George out to bring in any pregnant cows or newly born calves; the Herefords could drop their calves anytime after the third week of February and into late March. Instinctively, the expecting mothers would seek out shelter from the wind and elements taking refuge among small groves of trees or shallow ravines.

It was just such a ravine Finn was passing by, when a young Grizzly Bear suddenly emerged from a clearing near the edge of a pine coulee where it had been guarding its kill; a pregnant cow. The great beast charged towards Finn, badly spooking his horse so that it reared and whinnied in fright. The bear continued forward before suddenly pulling short and rearing up on its hind feet to its full height of nearly nine feet. Watching the horse and rider withdraw at the gallop, the bear realized its goal giving several final deep huffs and clacks of its massive jaws as a final warning. Vanishing into the underbrush, and returning to its kill, the bear managed to disperse a sizable flock of ravens, crows, and magpies from the carcass sending the disappointed scavengers to sit and quarrel among themselves upon the lower branches of the trees lining the small clearing.

Working on the ranch over the last year, the young cowboy had evolved to become a first-rate horseman. These skills enabled Finn to control his panicked mount and together they left the angry bear quickly behind. That's when disaster struck. In its frenzy to escape, the horse had plunged a front leg down into an old badger hole. Hearing a high-pitched scream, Finn simultaneously felt his spine slam and jar against his leather saddle. The horse's momentum carried the animal's bulk forward despite its front hoof being pinned below its body. Unable to free its hoof from the badger hole, the horse's leg bone broke with a resounding snap sending the horse tumbling downward into the earth taking Finn along with it. Striking the frozen earth, Finn's collarbone shattered and his shoulder dislocated. Yet far worse injury was to follow when the twelve hundred pound animal collapsed atop the man pinning him to the ground. Struggling to rise to its feet, the injured horse failed utterly, falling once again atop its luckless rider.

George had been riding on the far side of the ravine. Witnessing what had happened, he galloped over arriving at Finn's side only minutes later. There was little to do for Finn, his cousin was unconscious and approaching death. Shortly, the cow boss arrived on the scene in the company of another ranch hand. The boss quickly dispatched the wounded horse with his carbine and together the three managed to pull Finn free of the dead animal. Released, Finn managed to open his eyes and take a shallow breath. Sensing he was about to die, Finn spoke to the three men, saying that he bequeathed his wages and his share of the money saved to George before closing his eyes a final time.

The ranch owner, a fair and generous man, provided George with the remainder of Finn's earnings; then doubled the amount. Together with Finn's share of the money, George bought a quarter section near Pincher Creek as well as the tools and equipment needed to begin farming. He was preparing to leave Fort MacLeod in a couple of days when he spied a young dark haired beauty riding with whom he supposed were members of her family, atop a Red River cart.

Drawn by a single ox, the simple two-wheeled wooden cart creaked slowly along Main Street. Fashioned almost entirely of wood and containing little metal, the sturdy cart found itself in great favor by the Métis living in those settlements bordering the Red River far to the east. George watched the cart come to a stop in front of the black smith's shop. The driver, a swarthy man in his late thirties and of powerful build, stepped from the cart extending his hand to his wife and in turn assisting his daughters, beginning with the youngest.

Ignoring her father's extended hand; the eldest daughter remained frozen in place atop the wagon, her eyes fixed upon those of a young man who stood off a short distance. To George, it felt akin to a lightning strike. The girl, while still quite young, was very much a woman. Her rich brown curls flowed about her shoulders framing her dark complexion and pleasing features, there was little doubt that she was her father's daughter and of native ancestry. This was in contrast to those soft ice-blue eyes she clearly inherited from her flaxen haired mother.

Her father followed her stare back to a young man, one obviously quite enamored with his daughter. Grunting, the man cast George a disapproving look before returning to his daughter. He shook his outstretched arms before the girl, finally capturing her attention and helping her down from the cart. Grace's mother had seen the non-verbal exchange taking place between the two young people and smiled to herself thinking of how she and her husband had shared similar glances many years before.

The following spring, George and Grace were married. Loading up everything they possessed in the world, the couple journeyed westward from the Fort toward their new homestead. The road was little more than a rutted buffalo trail that soon became a soupy quagmire owing to the spring melt. Reaching their plot of land, they chose what they thought would be the best location for their future home. The homestead's site must be close enough to the creek to provide a convenient source of water, yet one occupying slightly higher ground should the creek flood during the spring runoff or during heavy rains.

Living in a small wall tent that first spring and summer, the young couple carved one by one foot squares of thick rooted earth from a selected square of prairie grass. Repositioning the heavy sod blocks within a rectangle, they managed to both clear what would become the home's dirt floor while forming the basic outline of their home's foundation. Repeating the heavy work, they obtained additional blocks of sod nearby, using these to build up their home's walls that soon rose to shoulder height. In the process, the couple established a cleared garden plot; the vegetables Grace grew that first summer would carry them through winter until the next spring.

George went about clearing a small strand of trees and the larger rocks from the first of twenty acres he intended to cultivate and plant with barley. The tree's lumber furnished the simple joists and rafters used to support the considerable weight of the home's sod roof. The rocks would form the cabin's fireplace, an essential feature required to warm the cabin during the colder months and allowing Grace to cook their meals indoors. The sod houses dotting the Canadian prairies took time and sweat to construct, but once built the thick walls and roof became natural insulators, providing the residents cool respite from the summer heat and a warm shelter from winter's chill.

The arduous, backbreaking work kept the couple busy from sunup to sundown. The long days allowed George to plant the small crop of barley just in time hoping the crop could mature before fall harvest. George and Grace were lucky. During the growing season, the crop enjoyed just enough rain and sunshine to ensure a good harvest providing a small amount of cash for any essentials as well as seed for next year's planting. Grace had planted their one-acre garden with green vegetables and rows of potatoes. Upon harvest, they stashed the summer's produce in a wood-lined root cellar George dug out during the hot summer months. George's hunting skills would provide venison for the table, while a small flock of chickens would provide eggs and a rare roast chicken dinner during the holidays. Reviewing their accomplishments, George and Grace felt they'd done exceedingly well, yet any thought of purchasing cattle, sheep, or building a small barn must wait until the following year.

Over the last five years, the Dunn's had managed to make good progress despite losing half their cowherd during the brutal winter of 1886/1887. Now once again it seemed their luck had changed for the worse. That morning George had walked his fields, quickly estimating what the railroad elevator in Fort MacLeod might give him for his thin, drought-ravaged crops. Returning to the cabin's porch, he found Grace busy at her mill, churning the day's milk into butter.

George sat himself down in his chair rather heavily before setting his faded, sweat brimmed Stetson atop a nearby table.

"It's not going to be enough is it." Grace stated resignedly.

"No, it is not. Certainly we'll get through the winter, but we won't have enough to pay for the spring seed, much less buy McClelland's bull." George shook his head. "Nor can we afford to carry debt; we'd lose the farm if our next crop isn't all it should be."

Deliberately cutting the conversation short Grace replied. "Well, I suppose I should prepare our luncheon." The woman turned intending to walk toward the cabin door nearly forgetting the butter mill she left sitting by her chair. Feeling somewhat defeated, George said nothing as his eyes followed her departure. Now inside and away from her husband's notice, she placed a hand on the slight swell of her belly. Her mind struggled with a singularly difficult problem. How was she going to tell George that they could expect their first child around the first week of next April?

The following morning, Grace accompanied George riding their buckboard wagon into the creek's settlement where they pulled up in front of a recently opened mercantile, a store and postal outlet jointly owned by Mr. James Schofield and Mr. Harry Hyde. The local settlers had cheered the store's opening since it spared them from making the otherwise necessary three-day trek to and back from Fort Macleod. A true general store, here the folks could buy a wide selection of goods making the difficult life on the southern prairies somewhat more comfortable. Pots and pans, canned goods, clothing, tobacco, coffee, sugar and flour and salt pork were only a few of the staples offered by the proprietorship.

A small bell tinkled above the store's doorframe announcing the Dunn's arrival and catching James Schofield standing atop a small ladder. Busily organizing soup cans along a shelf, he turned his head slightly. "Hi folks, be right with you."

"No hurry Jim." George closed the door tight checking the latch doing his best to shut out some of the dust carried in the strong nearly incessant winds of the last week or so. "Grace, why don't you look at some of those dresses over there? Pick out something suitable for a lady in your condition." George watched her eyes smile back at his. Grace turned toward the solitary clothes rack standing near the store's rear wall. Taking a short breath, she walked toward the general store's somewhat meager selection of various sized dresses, which hung in a kaleidoscope of calicos, plaids, and floral fabrics. Although unlikely to fit properly, Grace prided herself on her needlework.

George walked over to a side wall where several large wooden crates rested upon the raw plank floor. The tops of the crates lay along their sides, removed to display a varied collection of steel leg-hold traps along with their associated chains and hardware. Reaching into the nearest box, he removed a small trap George figured was sufficient to catch and hold an animal the size of a mink or martin. He rubbed a finger across the smooth arc shaped jaws noting the light film of oil atop its steel.

The oil ensured the rust free arrival of the traps while on their journey from eastern Canada.

Seeing George's interest in the items, Jim walked up beside George. "Won't find a finer set of traps in the world." The Newhouse brand was reputed to be among the best available. Manufactured in New York State, the brand's recent adoption by the Hudson Bay Company secured its footing in the market.

"They look ok, but then, I don't know much about trappin'." George set down the trap and picked up a sturdier version. "What do you figure this might hold?"

"That there? Ah, just hold on, I have some information that came with the traps." Jim walked behind the stores counter and returned moments later with a large page of heavy brown paper displaying the traps made by the company and their recommended usage. Jim ran a finger along a set of drawings comparing them to the item in George's hands. "Looks like that one's good for coyote, bobcat, and lynx. The next size up is for wolves, mountain lions, and such."

George glanced at several very large multi-toothed traps dangling from a large nail in the wall. "Bear?" He guessed aloud.

"Yup. Be a hell of a thing steppin' into that huh?" Jim chuckled.

George nodded in agreement. "If I was to buy some, what could I expect these things to set me back?

"Well... you know I haven't a clue. Harry just brought them into the store yesterday. He's out at his place right now, but he likely has them priced them in the ledger. Let me check."

"Obliged." George continued to browse while he waited.

"What do you think?" Grace had returned. She held up a calico print dress across her still slight figure, the material flowed and ballooned out on either side suggesting it would do nicely as her pregnancy matured.

A half hour or so later, George and Grace rode back to the farm. Anyone experienced in traveling over the rocky, rutted country roads and trails by buckboard, would agree the wagon was aptly named. At times, the jarring swaying motions of the wagon made speaking nearly impossible. They arrived at the farm and George set about unbridling the horse, ensuring it got a feedbag of oats before setting it loose in the coral.

George entered the cabin taking a seat upon a bench before their wooden plank table. Grace had laid a red and white checkered tablecloth overtop, covering the rough wood. She joined him, setting two mugs of fresh coffee before them. His wife wore a troubled expression; she'd seen him eyeing the traps in the store and hoped she wasn't correct in thinking what he might be saying to her next.

"Well, Jim gave me a pretty good price on a set of traps and irons." He glanced up at his wife's face as she fought to dispel the look of apprehension crossing her face. George continued. "I know this isn't what you were hoping, but... Well Grace, if I even do half as well as Ned Appleton did last season we could be sitting pretty this coming spring."

Grace knew better than question her husband; it was a man's world, and a woman's job was to live within it as best she could. "How long will you be gone?"

"I'd be leaving 'bout the end of October, come back early March some time. I guess it depends upon my luck. You never know how things are going to be 'til you get out there."

"I don't want to say it, but husband, you don't know much about running a trap line." Grace stated frankly.

"I know. Jim Schofield told me that Ned Appleton's going out again this season. Could be he wants for some company, at least as far as traveling out to the Livingstone Range. After that we'd split up and run our own lines." George stared a hole in the bottom of his coffee mug. "I hate to leave you alone Grace. Is there anyway Erma might come out from Fort MacLeod and stay here with you?"

"I'd have to write my father and you'd have to travel out to get her, unless you convince Jim or Henry to bring her out with them after they go into the fort for supplies." Grace's sister had only turned fourteen, but even so, the girl was handy about the house and would prove welcome company during the dark winter months.

A snowy October 23rd arrived along with Grace's sister Erma. Her sister had traveled the thirty-four miles by wagon together with Mr. Hyde and a young N.W.M.P. constable, a replacement for another man at the post. The constable had joined them in Fort MacLeod having ridden south from Calgary and after checking in with the Fort's commandant.

Erma had arrived at the general store about noon, and well before her anticipated arrival nearer to supper. Hyde hadn't charged Erma anything for the trip out, the road was long and he was grateful for the company, his eldest son who usually made the trip with him had fallen ill with a fever. Far from sitting about waiting for George and Grace, Erma had made herself busy, dusting the store shelves and counter, straightening clothes, and tidying up where she could. Henry Hyde was impressed and said so, adding that if Grace approved, he could employ the girl in the store one day per week.

The trip out to the farm along the snow packed roads had done a lot to smooth the buckboards ride. Grace drove the horse, while the sisters talked and gabbed about family happenings and the latest news in Fort MacLeod. The horse pulled the wagon into the farmyard just in time for the women to see George laying the last armful of split log firewood beneath a lean-to he'd built on the lee side of their barn. Out of the wind, and hopefully free of drifted snow, it would make the woman's task accessing the several cords of pine, birch and aspen he'd managed to stockpile over the past several weeks a bit easier.

Early the next morning saw George kiss and hug Grace for several long moments before opening the door and leaving the cabin. Grace stood in the open doorway watching her husband pick up the straps of a light sled packed with the necessary supplies; with luck, it would be full and bulging with furs upon his return. Ned Appleton's place lay several miles distant, George would arrive in an hour or so. From there the two men would trek North by West for nearly a week, heading deep into the foothills and among the smaller peaks and lonely valleys of the Livingstone Mountains beyond.

Grace waited until George had traveled beyond her sight. Slowly closing the door, Grace's chest heaved and her shoulder leaned into the doorframe. Shortly sagging with emotion, she regained a measure of composure before turning to see Erma's concerned face. Noticing Grace's tear lined face, Erma immediately approached her sister and the two women hugged for several minutes before disengaging.

Grace turned toward the small wood burning stove setting a soot-blacked kettle atop one of the stove's rounded iron plates. "I think this calls for a pot of tea, don't you?" She pointed to a cupboard. "George bought us some sweet biscuits this week; he's such a dear..." Her eyes glistened and filled with tears once more. It would be a long worrisome winter.

Iska

Iska found herself driven eastwards and leaving her usual haunts through necessity rather than choice. The recent summer's wild fires had stolen both her kits while reducing much of her range to little more than smoldering ash. To stay on would mean starvation. Several days earlier, she struck out in search of new territory. Passing overhead and carried upon a southerly breeze, the last of the wood smoke turned the sun to bronze.

Iska's path wound steadily eastward passing through the old growth boreal forests. Not wandering aimlessly, she sought out a familiar scent, that of her previous mate several years earlier. Although no longer in estrous or interested in mating, there was still a slim chance, he might tolerate her presence should she remain on the outskirts of his range during the coming winter.

Others of her kind, and strangers to herself would view her arrival as a violation of their territory, the available prey, and of course mating opportunities. If Iska possessed sufficient strength, she might drive another from its range and take control of their range, but this eventuality was highly unlikely. While fleeing the conflagration, a fiery branch fell from above striking her haunches and rendering her incapable of moving for several minutes while the fire roared and swept through the forest canopy above her. If it hadn't been for an unexpected change in the winds direction, she would not have survived. As it was she crept from of the fire's path remaining holed up in a rocky crag for the better part of a week while she healed and recovered enough strength to continue her trek. It would take some time for her badly singed fur to regain its normally lustrous condition.

The female wolverine or angeline was both fast and nearly fearless. Her small eyes and a pair of short rounded ears extended above her rounded, broad head. Despite their diminutive size, she possessed exceptional sight and hearing. Her short powerful limbs each armed with five long claws allowed her to climb trees, steep mountain slopes, and even icy cliffs with relative ease. Not a large animal, only the size of a medium dog, her short legs and long body provided her a low center of gravity that she used to advantage when attacked. Whenever threatened, Iska's body would hug the ground, her snarls, and growls accompanied by a foul disgusting odor secreted from her scent glands giving notice to cougars, wolves, and even grizzly bears as to what they faced. Quite often, the larger animals would retreat rather than risk attack. Forced to fight when cornered, the fifty to seventy pound animals were all sharp teeth and claws. Spinning about like a whirling dervish, these animals dealt out far more damage than they received - their unusual strength far out of proportion to their size.

North American Wolverine

As wolverines went, Iska was a fine specimen. Her upper body and back covered in rich dark brown fur, she sported a pale buff stripe that ran back along her powerful shoulders and sides ending in a patch above her short bushy tail. Unlike many other individuals, Iska also displayed a prominent white patch on her throat and chest, though few of her kind would ever see this feature. Iska and others of her kind were solitary animals, the adult wolverines coming together to mate between May and August. Shortly after co-joining, they would go their separate ways often never meeting again. The females enjoyed a converse relationship, one shared between a mother and her young, the kits staying by her side up to several years before moving on and establishing their own ranges.

Iska generally had no difficulty finding her usual prey, that usual being pretty much anything she could kill or scavenge, but the lands she now passed through were increasingly strange. She continued eastward following along a riverbank. To either side of her, the rocky windswept crags pressed close, crowding the pine and spruce into a dense, nearly impenetrable underbrush. What had recently been a broad valley formed by the shallow, meandering river had constricted to little more than a narrow pass. The once docile river transforming itself into a raging torrent, its angry waters crashing against the time-rounded granite boulders embedded with the streambed before the rapids fell abruptly into a series of white foamed cascades and waterfalls spilling into deep blue green pools, whose waters still churned and boiled with a dangerous violence.

Iska navigated the thick brush on either side of the river, careful not to stray too near the sharp ledge. Her course led steadily downward for several hours. Finally, the river's narrows widened and the speed of its current relented when the steep mountainsides once again parted to reveal a vast U-shaped valley. The valley's side's scraped smooth by the passing glaciers of another age; it now wore a mantle of emerald verdure. In a few places, the darker greens of the predominant conifers lay broken where sparse stands of aspen and birch took hold and grew in hollows, flats, and clearings, the trees announcing autumn's arrival within their leaves of burnished gold.

She moved into the valley and upward along the northern wall. Iska's kind enjoyed the elevated countryside, although they'd venture lower during those times when winter's blast drove their prey into the valley seeking grasses, shrubs, and shelter from the icy, biting winds at higher altitudes. Iska paused sticking her sensitive nose upward and into the breeze; something nearby smelled delicious, but where was it coming from? The angeline began moving in ever widening circles, her nose twitching and bidding her to follow the odor of blood and offal the led to a well-used game trail. Her sensitive ears told her other predators lay in the direction of her food; she'd have to move silently upwind while taking stock of the situation.

The Grey wolves had made the kill the previous day. Surprising a small mule deer doe, they ran it to ground dispatching the luckless animal in their usual gory fashion, ripping it to pieces in a frenzied rush. The wolves were few in number, a much smaller pack than normally found in the area and consisting of an Alpha male, his mate, and two younger cousins. The wolves would feed another day or two on the carcass before moving on. For now, they stretched out among the pine needles and moss, contentedly dozing and sunning themselves in the afternoon's sunbeams that occasionally glittered and broke through the forest canopy to warm the forest floor.

Climbing upon a nearby log, Iska couldn't believe her luck. Although she hadn't recovered all of her strength, her willpower and ferocity hadn't dimmed an iota. She knew she was more than a match for the contented animals basking in the dappled sunlight below her. Iska would begin her assault by targeting the Alpha male; a quick twenty-foot rush through the brush would see her fangs and front claws raking his hindquarters. The sudden vicious attack mixed with her snarls, growls and the pungent stench secreted from her glands would announce her unexpected arrival.

Iska thrust herself forward with speed and intent, striking the wolf with unbridled fury. The Alpha male bolted, howling in pain and surprise, he turned in tight circles, not yet certain in which direction the attack was coming from. Iska hugged the ground during her attack; her thick fur and superbly muscled back would act as an effective armor against an enemy's teeth or claws should any choose to fight. Instinctively, the Alpha male and his mate backed away a short distance until they could evaluate the threat, while their young cousins had already decided they weren't having any part of the situation and were even now loping into the forest and fleeing the conflict.

The Alpha female took the initiative charging at Iska head on before stopping dead in her tracks, it was merely a bluff to test the wolverines resolve. The angeline didn't surrender an inch and stood her ground facing down the pair of wolves who snarled, their lips drawn back in a display their long incisors. It was now time for Iska to signal her objective. Still facing the two wolves, she shuffled almost crablike; moving sideways until she reached what remained of the deer carcass. Once there the wolverine stood over the kill growling and snapping her jaws in challenge.

The standoff continued for several long minutes, the longer the interval the more likely Iska was to prevail. For their part, the wolves hunger had been sated, there was no urgent need for them to feed, even if there was, they knew the odds were against a final victory. The female wolverine was one tough customer, even if the greys were present in larger numbers; there was a good chance some wolves would find themselves badly injured in the conflict. Any injury in the wilderness, even one not immediately resulting in death could degrade a predator's ability to hunt or keep up with its pack resulting in the animal's starvation. There are times when discretion truly is the better option to valor. The grey wolves turned about and vanished into the forest.

Iska fed on the carcass until her hunger abated before taking the deer's hind leg in her powerful jaws and effortlessly pulling the entire carcass into the deep brush past the edge of the clearing. Here she would rest and remain for several days until she had consumed the entire carcass. Once regaining her full strength, Iska would explore her new surroundings. Whatever destiny presented her, it would determine if she would stay or move on.

ONWARD TOWARD THE LIVINGSTONE RANGE

George and Ned Appleton moved westward, tracing a route along the southern banks of the Crow's Nest River. Over the last six days, the weather had been more co-operative than they could have hoped. The nights were certainly crisp, but not uncomfortably so. Neither man felt compelled to erect their small wall tents, relying instead on only a modest lean-to; little more than a windbreak the makeshift shelter would shield the two from a sudden snowfall. The weather in this part of the country could be as fickle as a woman and as unpredictable as a mother grizzly bear. They would enjoy those final shortening days of October before November's chilly bluster arrived, the harbinger of winter's dark, icy embrace.

They had made excellent progress covering nearly ten miles per day. While the distance traveled may appear to some people to be rather slow, others who knew better would realize any number of factors governed their pace. The weight of their sleds, the variable elevation of the terrain, the number and depth of creek beds and shallow ravines, and finally, even the characteristics of the snow which itself changed by the hour. Throughout the day, the runners of their sleds, despite their lower surfaces freshly waxed each morning, might find the men pulling their sleds smoothly across a crusty surface, half-buried within unexpected powder or worst of all and thankfully rare, floundering within a sticky, semi-solid morass. At those times, the sled's polished runners seemed glued to the surface of the trail. One of those times occurred during the previous afternoon march, when George and Ned found themselves struggling and near exhaustion having covered less than a single mile by nightfall.

The following morning found the men's vigor renewed. Breakfast consisted of coffee and several bowls of hot porridge fortified with nuts, raisins, and berries - a trail mix of sorts and one that would provide the energy necessary for the day's travel. Finishing their meal, the men waxed the sleds runners and prepared to break camp, their boots crunching noisily upon the thin crust of refrozen snow found the men eager to proceed.

By noon the men approached a crossroads in the trail. A four-foot high, rock piled obelisk stood to one side while a broad wooden arrow pointed to a breach among the snowy peaks far beyond to the west. Nearby a small sign, its carved lettering stained with faded black paint, proclaimed the way forward belonged a section of the "British Kutanie Pass." If followed, the trail would continue westward leading the traveller into the first of a series of steep narrow valleys winding their way through the various mountain ranges before finally ending upon reaching the shores of the Pacific Ocean. This passageway, though long known to the many indigenous tribes residing within the mountainous lands, found itself seldom travelled. The pass was both treacherous and difficult to navigate no matter the season, although it did allow for limited trade and of course, the inevitable tribal conflicts that came with it.

In thousands of years long past, the ocean levels had dropped as miles deep glacial ice sheets developed and spread far afield across the northern hemisphere. Within North America, the Laurentide ice sheet imprisoned the eastern half of the continent in its grip, while to the west the Rocky Mountains bore the full weight of her Cordilleran counterpart. Capturing and imprisoning incalculable volumes of fresh water within the glacial ice, the oceans diminished, exposing a thin archipelago; a chain of low rising islands linking prehistoric Asia to that of North America. The bridge was temporary, though if only considered within geologic terms. For two and one half million years the glaciers would ebb and re-grow. This constant seesaw resulted in the ocean levels rising and falling leaving the archipelago to appear then disappear once more beneath the waves of a rising ocean.

Being near the warm ocean currents, the climate was for the most part temperate, allowing vegetation to grow and flourish during the summer months while allowing ice age mammals to migrate southward during winter. The frozen ice flows connecting the islands to create the famed "Bering Strait land bridge." As is the nature of all life on the planet, flora and fauna ceaselessly seek to expand their numbers and increase their range. So to, the ancient peoples who followed their prey fell into locked step moving ever southward and following the Pacific west coast. Still their progress measured not in years, but in tens and hundreds of centuries.

George and Ned removed their shoulder straps, looping them across the sleds before looking out to the various directions of the compass. The western trail continued toward the mountain pass, first named by Captain Palliser, an Irish explorer and geographer of considerable renown. To the south, their eyes could make out little more than patchy game trails meandering across the higher ground. It was to the northwest where their objective lay.

George took a swig from his canteen stuffing it beneath the tent and bedding atop his sled. "How much further you figure?"

Ned scratched his chin whiskers and calculated. "I figure maybe another couple days north." Sitting upon his sled, he removed his light glove and fished about within an inside coat pocket. His hand emerged grasping a thin metal case. Opening the case, Ned removed a cigarette before deftly striking a match and setting the small flame to the tobacco taking several quick puffs. The cigarette represented one of the few and rarely enjoyed luxuries the man had carefully rationed out over the next four months.

Ned exhaled a thin cloud of smoke that quickly dissipated in the breeze. "After that, west along a creek bed heading up into the Porcupine Hills, depending upon the weather we'll hit Cauldron Peak. We'll rest up, maybe for a day or so, after that we have a good climb ahead of us. There's a high mountain meadow running along the south edge of the Cauldron's base, about five miles west the land drops into forest." He took another puff, the end of the cigarette brightened to a cherry red shortly before falling back into a grey smolder. Ned stood, knocked off the lit end of his smoke, and then carefully stored the half-finished cigarette within its case, saving the butt for later.

George stated flatly, "It'll be good to rid myself of this sled. My arms and shoulders are aching, to say nothing of my back." Despite being young and in good shape, the journey tasked both men; each looked forward to establishing their winter camp.

"And that my good sir, is where you and I part company. My line circles a good twenty miles to the south of the creek, your line shall be whatever you choose, but will swing off to the north." Ned leaned over and retrieved the padded canvass straps fastened to his sled slipping them over one shoulder at a time. "Well, no time like the present. Shall we press on?"

George followed Ned's lead and together they tramped northward across a snowy path, their travels taking them along a demarcation line separating the Alberta foothills to the west and the vast western plains to the east. As he walked, George's thoughts strayed to his farm then fell upon Grace and their unborn child; suddenly he felt himself exceedingly grateful that Erma was back home to lend Grace a hand.

Other questions kept nagging at him with every step he took. Had he made the right choice venturing into the tall timber for the winter? Should he have remained at home trusting to luck that he and Grace would have enough money to plant a crop, enough to carry them through the summer until next year's harvest? Would the harvest be good? What if the rains failed to arrive just as they had this past year? He shook his head, reminding himself that both he and Grace had asked themselves each of these questions and many more before finally concluding that George's idea of running a winter trap line was likely the best, if not the only way to guarantee a future for themselves and their family.

MEANWHILE BACK HOME

Grace stood back several feet distant from a small oval mirror affixed to the wall, now able to view her entire body. Erma watched her sister smooth her palms across the growing swell of her lower belly. Grace's face wore a peculiar expression, somewhere between a smile and a frown. Erma guessed that while the woman was pleased with her health and presumably that of her unborn child, Grace had either badly miscalculated her original April due date or perhaps she might be carrying twins.

"I'm more than a couple of months along aren't I?" Grace didn't so much ask as state.

Erma walked to her side and positioned her hand atop Grace's which continued to rest upon her tummy. "I'm guessing three months, maybe more." Erma decided to take a more optimistic approach. "You do remember that this is your first?" She cocked her head to one side while watching her sister's face in the mirror. "Do you remember how big Aunt Cindy got when she was only four months gone, everyone figured she was either carrying triplets or that she and Ed hadn't bothered waiting for their wedding date or ... well you know?"

"Wasn't that quite the scandal? Thank God Cindy delivered a full month later than her wedding."

Erma added. "I would bet Ed was relieved as well!"

"You know I overheard Father telling Mother that very thing!" The young women giggled and smiled. Grace turned to Erma; her face indicating her concern had lifted, at least for the moment. "You're probably right, I might just be... bigger than most?"

The women went about their chores and working together, they had finished by noon.

Grace washed their few dishes, heating water on the wood stove and pouring it over the plates and mugs within an oval washbasin sitting atop a bench set aside of the cabin's door. Having set the sparse tableware within a small trunk set beneath the bed that she and Erma now shared, she swept the dirt floor with a homemade straw broom before inspecting the walls. Finding new holes and cracks, she pushed small stones and wooden chips between the pieces of sod hoping to prevent the mice entry.

While Grace busied herself with her own tasks, Erma tended the animals. After milking their cow, she placed the warm half pail of milk on the porch; churning the milk to butter could wait for now. She walked the cow from the barn and into the corral where two steers waited. Returning within the small structure, she lifted a large rectangular bale of hay from a stack piled near the barn's back wall. Struggling with her heavy load, she dropped it along the corral's fence; cutting the bale string, she tossed double handfuls of the hay towards the expectant cattle. She'd wait until evening before shoveling a silage mixture of oats, corn, and barley into their cattle trough. On her final trip to the barn, Erma placed a thin brick of alfalfa beneath one arm and grabbed a small pail of silage, which she carried over to a separate wired enclosure that housed the sheep and goats.

Typical 1880's Barn

Grace was walking back from the creek, holding a heavy pail of water in each hand. Erma scurried toward her sister. "Just what do you think you're doing? Silly goose, this is why George asked me to stay with you!"

"I'm pregnant; not feeble." Grace set the pails on the ground and looked upward. Over the last several hours, banks of low grey cloud had replaced the morning's previously azure blue sky. Now off to the western horizon, the sky had taken on a decidedly navy hue signalling that an abrupt change in weather may be on its way.

"Erma, I think we should hitch up ol' Red up to the buckboard." It was high time that she and her sister paid a visit to the mercantile to pick up some necessary supplies. Grace chided herself for having put off the short trip this past week. She hoped they could avoid whatever weather might be coming their way before the trip home.

By the time the women arrived in town, the previously balmy temperature had already fallen. The gentle southern breeze had vanished. Changing direction, the wind had picked up, now gusting out of the northwest. Using a hand to hold her hat atop her head, Erma stepped down from the wagon quickly tying Red to a hitch rail in front of the general store.

Jim Schofield stepped out from the store's doorway, quickly walking toward several wicker baskets laying displayed upon the store's veranda. An unexpected gust of wind caught the light baskets sending them tumbling across the wooden planks. Seeing the baskets attempting their escape, Erma quickly stepped up, trapping the hand baskets between her legs.

Jim bent taking the items in tow. "Just in the nick of time! Thank you Erma." Looking over one shoulder and casting an eye westward Jim remarked. "You ladies best get yourselves inside, we'll have you sorted and on your way shortly."

The girls stepped inside and approached the counter. A line of candy jars sat upon the smooth wood stained countertop. On the wall behind the counter, were shelves of various sizes. The lower, wider shelves held the canned goods, those further up displayed lighter inventory, or items commanding higher prices - spices, tobacco, liquor, and spirits. A breeze wafted in from the rear of the store. Standing near an open back door, Harry Hyde kicked it closed with the back of his boot heel, his arms holding a case of canned beans and another of canned peaches overtop. Saying to no one in particular Harry set down his load. "Getting a bit chilly out there."

Jim worked his way behind his counter and set both palms flat on its surface. "Ok Grace, what would you be needing today?" Working off a small piece of paper, Grace read off a list of items that Jim and Harry quickly set about gleaning from the mercantile shelves, drawers, and boxes. Within five minutes or less, the men escorted the women out the door, loading up a wooden box onto the rear of the buckboard containing their purchase, then helping each woman into their wagon.

"Thanks Jim; Harry." Grace smiled and nodded to the men while she tightened her bonnet about her head. The wind tugged at her shawl and dress.

"Blowing in quick! Now you ladies get toward home right away. "Harry urged. The first flakes of snow had just appeared in the now bitingly cold wind. "Would you like one of us to escort you home... be no bother at all?"

"No, thanks for the offer Harry, but we're only a couple of miles away." The men waved to the women then quickly re-entered the store.

By the time Grace and Erma had arrived home, the snow was already flying thick. Driven by a ferocious wind it stung their faces and hands, numbing any portion of exposed skin. The women turned their faces from the blast, shielding their eyes; now reduced to little more than mere slits. The left side of Red's thick winter coat lay covered with windblown snow, its colour had slowly paled from dull ochre to light beige.

Entering the farmyard, Grace didn't pause, but drove the horse and buckboard to its regular spot. Climbing down and running toward the front of the wagon, she felt her boots sink into three inches of newly fallen snow. Quickly working with stiffened ice-cold hands, she fought against the frosty leather and metal, finally succeeding in releasing the horse from its tethers.

After running the box of supplies into the cabin, Erma returned and stood beside the open barn door, she held it open watching Grace's approach, leading the horse by its halter. The wide door bucked in Erma's grip. Suddenly caught in the gale, it threatened to close despite her best efforts, but the slight woman somehow managed to keep it open until Grace and the horse had stepped inside. For the next ten minutes, the women frantically worked leading the unwilling livestock into the barn and securing them within their stalls or pens. Having fed the animals, they firmly latched the barn's doors and openings before racing across the snowy farmyard, their shawls tightly drawn about their head and shoulders while the wild blizzard's winds howled in their ears.

Shielded within the cabin, and free of the ferocious winds, Erma went about lighting the kerosene lamps, dispelling the afternoon's inclement gloom. Grace checked the stovepipe's flue ensuring it was clear then set a match to the kindling she'd expertly stacked within the iron stove. The sod cabin had succeeded in its primary task, one of hoarding the midmorning's heat. Its thick walls and the six-inch slabs of prairie grass set atop the roof's planks provided excellent insulation from both summer heat and winters chill. A quarter hour later, Grace and Erma sat at the kitchen table holding steaming cups of tea while staring out through the cabin's single small glass window.

Tornados of snowflakes whipped and churned their way about the abandoned farmyard. Peering outside, the women found themselves unable to discern the boundary between earth and sky - the "white-out" making it nearly impossible to make out anything except the barn's hazy outline only some fifty feet distant.

Grace mentally kicked herself; she should never have taken the chance of riding into town. There was nothing lacking in the home that couldn't have waited for better weather! Neither of them had been properly dressed! Had the whiteout struck while they were still plodding along the road, it was quite possible, if not likely, that the women wouldn't have arrived. They'd have frozen to death somewhere in the blinding snow, unsure of what direction they were walking, the trail home hidden beneath the deepening snows, and the wind quickly stealing whatever heat their bodies retained.

Now warm and snuggling within a heavy knit wool sweater, Grace gratefully took a sip of her tea. A moment later her cup suddenly slipped and dangled in her grasp, the tea spilling upon the table and the cup nearly dropping atop her saucer as her thoughts darted toward the wilderness and what dangers her husband might be facing. My God! And what of George!

THE TRAILHEAD CAMP

Throughout the night, a waterproof oilcloth tarp snapped and cracked like a whip. The gale force winds doing their best to rip the tarp free of the hemp ropes securing it tightly above George's canvas wall tent. At times, the wind would calm to a whisper, as if waiting to regain its strength before resuming its assault. During those occasions when the winds diminished, George would venture outside to check the guy wires and each time he'd find the snow drifts rising ever higher along the windward side of his shelter. Brushing excess snow from the tarp, he paid special attention to the soot-blacked chimney pipe poking out above the small pavilion. The slender pipe panted out a thin stream of grey wood smoke that quickly dissipated in the frigid breeze.

As cold and inhospitable as it was outside the tent, the inside temperature was almost balmy in comparison. The small wood stove provided enough warmth to prevent his water from freezing, while his bedroll lay atop an eighteen inch high, pine log frame. George had covered the logs in a deep layer of moss taken from the forest floor, overall, George slept comfortably in his makeshift bed. A small candle burned within a slender glass mantle while his two larger kerosene lanterns remained unlit beneath his bed. A burning lantern within the tent would not only produce an evil smelling, oily smoke, but if improperly vented those same vapors could easily asphyxiate a man as he slept. Besides the small candle would furnish all the light he needed inside the tent during the long winter nights.

George opened a corner of the tent flap and peered out into the dark. Twenty feet distant sat a second wall tent. A dim flickering glow on the tents walls and Ned's deep snores and whistles, told George the man was completely oblivious to the weather. George checked his watch; it was nearly six a.m. This time of year the sun rose late and retired early, especially in a camp set among the mountains and deep forest.

Two days earlier the men had arrived at what Ned had referred to as the trailhead; although in reality, it was but last year's camp and the beginnings of the meandering trap line Ned had marked and committed to memory. The rough circuit wound through twenty miles or more of forest, ridge, valley, and bog; on average would take him three days to complete.

The trap lines course changed and evolved throughout the entire season; as one area grew depleted of fur bearing animals, Ned had ventured into slightly new ranges. Still, the man stuck to the "three day" rule, unwilling to venture further afield since trapped animals were often discovered by winged scavengers and other predators leaving his efforts all for not. There was also the chance he might sustain an injury, or that bad weather or severe cold might strike during his rounds. If he were too far afield from main camp, there was always the chance he might not make it back.

George was impressed with Ned's choice of a winter camp. The trailhead had everything necessary for a long stay. The ground where they placed the tents was a flat clearing sheltered from the prevailing north winds by towering spruce, pine and a small stand of aspen. A small pond of clear, mountain fed waters collected in a shallow depression at the confluence of two small creeks. Each stream flowed down an opposing forested slope until they found common ground and merged to form the pond before draining out and running northwest, tracing the gentle slopes about the western base of Cauldron Mountain.

They'd dug a fire pit beneath the low boughs of a large bushy spruce that would provide excellent shelter from wind and snow. The pit lay only ten or twelve feet from the edge of the pond. The men didn't stop the backbreaking work until they'd dug nearly four feet into the earth. At this depth, they'd struck the local water table. Here the water pooled slightly but refused to rise any more than a quarter inch higher above the exposed earth. George and Ned lined the bottom and sides of the depression with gravel and flat rocks gathered beneath the moss beds and streams. The reason for doing so was an important one.

Should a fire burn within a pit over the course of days or weeks, it would eventually dry out the soil allowing heat to pass deeper into the earth. At some point, the intense heat may reach the roots of trees or bushes, igniting their wood and causing them to smolder. Completely undetectable from above the forest floor, the fire will slowly continue to burn as it consumes the root, moving through the soil and acting like a slow burning fuse. Upon reaching that part of the tree growing above ground, discovering a renewed source of oxygen, the smolder burst into flame. Depending upon the time of year, the moisture present, the dryness of the surrounding tinder, and of course the strength and direction of the wind; you just might find yourself in the midst of a raging wild fire.

Having set camp, the men went about knocking down several deadfalls located within a hundred yards of camp and stacking several cords of firewood beneath an oilcloth tarp weighted down with heavy rocks. The dead trees had likely stood for years, and exposed to the elements, they'd become bone dry, once cut, sawn and split, they were an excellent source of well-cured firewood. This said; the men took great care when felling the deadfalls; these larger trees were also nicknamed "widow makers" and for good reason.

The dead tree's internal structure was brittle and weak. A widow maker's main trunk had the unfortunate tendency of occasionally breaking free of its stump altogether, sending a ton or more of wood jutting out in unpredictable directions. Now if that direction happened to align with yours, well...

During the night, the storm moved past the trailhead and eastward toward the foothills. If it hadn't blown itself out, the weather front would arrive in Pincher Creek no later than noon. The fallen snow would greet the men upon waking, but meanwhile they dreamt of their women back home; clad within plaid cotton nightgowns and cozily tucked beneath heavy quilts.

Throwing open the tent flap, George stooped down, his feet sinking into a shallow drift of newly fallen snow. The early morning rays of the sun struck the highest peaks of the mountains surrounding the camp, bathing them in the dawn's pastels. George stood tall and took a deep breath found the unsullied morning air interlaced with the sharp fragrance of the nearby pines and the underlying woody scent of this autumn's recently fallen leaves. Lifting his gaze revealed the uppermost snowy crags and towering peaks; their resplendent brilliant whites scraping the ice blue sky, while pinks, soft violets, and deep shades of purple draped the still shadowed forest slopes. It promised to be a fine day.

Moments later Ned appeared, arching his back and stretching his arms wide. "A might breezy last night." He stated nonchalantly.

"Aye, just a might." George chuckled as he turned and drew in and tied the tent flaps. "Bit of breakfast before we head out?"

"Coffee first, need to clean out the cobwebs." Ned replied. Standing at the fire pit, he used a pine bough to sweep out a small skiff of the previous night's snow exposing several blackened, half-burnt logs. "You'll follow me about my line 'til midmorning, I'll show you how and where to set your snares and traps. After that, you can head back here and head out this afternoon to mark your own line. Don't need two fellows traipsing along the line laying down our scent and disturbing anything more than we need to. "

The men donned their snowshoes and slung rifles across their backs. Ned smiled holding out a leather harness in George's direction attached to a small sled loaded with whatever equipment and supplies were required for the short two or three day circuit while setting the early season trap line. "I'll supply the knowhow, you gotta tow the line." George willingly took the harness draping it about his shoulders. He couldn't wait to learn the ropes and get set his own line.

Ned had the patience, woodlore, and experience necessary to be a good teacher while George was an avid student. Ned explained where and how to set the various types of traps, snares, and deadfalls that would provide the men the opportunity to earn a decent profit. They take the best furs and pelts in the early to mid part of the season. At such times, the animals were still in their prime, their fur thick, their bodies fattened for winter. Depending upon their luck, their lines might yield a sufficient harvest allowing for their return as early as late January.

The men traversed the snow-covered terrain rather slowly. Ned's original line had become choked with this summer's brush, fallen logs and the like requiring them to navigate and pick their way past the various obstacles. Almost noon, Ned stopped and cursed.

His original trail had narrowed as it followed along the base of a rocky ridge that rose up to a height of nearly forty feet to his left, while to his right, was the edge of a wide marshy bog. That convenient trail no longer existed. Sometime this year, a thick slab of the limestone forming the cliff side had split and shifted forward. Gravity had sent a tumbling cascade of stone and rock crashing downward and obliterating the trail while creating an impassable jumble of jagged, broken debris extending outward into the bog.

The way forward across dry land was impassible and trying to navigate safely across the marsh would be far too dangerous. The subzero cold of the previous January had seen Ned attempt a short cut across the bog. Before daring to venture forth, Ned located a twig bare branch. Probing his way forward, Ned stabbed the branch into the snow having confidence that he ventured out onto solid ice thinking its surface would bear at least his weight and probably far more. His assumptions were incorrect and nearly fatal; in some spots, a warm spring welled upward feeding the bog from a deep aquifer. Ned quickly found himself nearly up to his waist and caught within an icy quagmire. Had he not been holding the branch, he would have been unable to brace himself and lift his body from the sucking ooze. Instead he would have joined the countless other men who throughout the ages had simply disappeared in the high country, never leaving any trace of their passing.

We can't go forward from here. We'll have to go back a half mile, climb the backside of this ridge; follow it past this point then hike back down to the trail." Ned shook his head. "Well, there goes the rest of the morning."

The men turned about retracing their steps. When they'd reached the western base of the limestone ridge Ned looked at his friend. "No sense in you hanging about George, taught you just about everything I know about trappin; now the rest is up to you." He held out his hand taking the harness from George, they shook their ungloved hands.

"Thanks Ned. I really mean it! Sure couldn't see Grace and me keeping the place if I didn't earn some extra money somehow." He smiled and adjusted his rifle sling across his back.

"Learning to run a trapline is pretty much just trial and error. You'll find out soon enough. Just remember to watch yourself, don't take any chances, always play it safe."

"I will, don't worry." George began to turn away.

Ned added. "Remember, if you do run into trouble..."

"Fire three shots and wait. If you don't show up in half a day or so, fire three more."

"You got it. See you back at the trailhead in three days time. You can sketch out your line in case I need to find you." Ned gave a quick wave then took his first steps that would lead him to the top of the ridge.

George arrived back at the trailhead in the early afternoon and ate a small meal before preparing his sled. Loading snare wire, bait and traps, an oilcloth tarp, his bedroll, food and a single change of clothing in case what he wore became wet for some reason, he was almost ready to go. Checking his compass before he left, George now tramped along a well-used game trail that led north, tracing the base of Cauldron Mountain. Over a space of days he'd cut west, then south, and finally east while returning to the trailhead camp.

Moving forward, every so often he'd clearly notch a tree trunk near the trail with the small hatchet always carried on his belt or sometimes build a cairn of rocks and stones. The pile of stones would not only aid as a trail marker but would function as a small emergency cache in which he'd place a tin can holding matches, candles and several rounds of rifle ammunition at its base. While it was unlikely a woodsman would get lost on a sunny day or a clear night, should the skies turn a dull grey or if snow began falling, you could soon find yourself turned about if you didn't recognize the terrain.

The countryside George chose to run his line appeared to combine all the essential elements, especially when finding his path criss-crossed in many places by the tracks of various animals. In some places, scat littered the ground near possible burrows, in others; the snow laid beaten flat by the frequent passage of little paws. Here he'd set unbaited snares along the trail. Moving along the pathways the small animals might trip and catch their bodies up within the disguised or well-hidden wire.

In other places, depending upon the kind and size of the animals George guessed were responsible for the tracks and signs, he's set baited steel-jawed traps for the larger game. For smaller predators, he constructed dead falls, propping up a heavy rock or log using nothing more than several wooden sticks. Ned had shown George how to build a simple, yet highly effective trap.

Taking a small branch measuring about eight to ten inches long, George snapped it in two pieces, shaving the broken edges smooth and shaping them so they slanted slightly inward, these would act to support the killing weight directly above the baited trigger. Selecting a smaller stick that would act as the trigger, George sliced one end flat and thin, wedging that thin edge between the centers of the larger fitted sticks. While holding all three carefully fitted pieces steady with one hand, George slowly lowered a heavy rock or log atop the larger sticks, creating a precarious balance that would fail with the slightest pressure exerted upon the trigger. Taking a small bit of meat, he positioned the bait atop the other end of the twig. Should a small animal disturb the trigger in any way, moving it ever so slightly in any direction, the wedged ends of the larger sticks would shift and part causing the rock to fall and crush the animal below.

There were a number of different versions of this deadfall, some slightly more complex; some designs may be preferred over others depending upon the location and animal targeted.

A "Figure 4" Deadfall

Happily, George found the terrain more forgiving than that of Ned's. His pathway through the forest valley took him along narrow streams or across shallow, partially frozen brooks that he crossed with ease. He made good time, completing what he estimated to be his first twenty plus mile circuit in little more than several days. He was pleased with what he thought he'd accomplished. Now he'd have to wait a day or so before striking out, retracing his route, and discovering whatever bounty awaited him.

NEW RANGES

Iska began exploring her new home travelling in a large clockwise circle measuring approximately fifteen to twenty miles in diameter. Along the way, she scent marked the outer boundaries of her range. Nearly completing the circuit, she knew what species of animals were present, and more importantly other wolverines living in the territory, yet so far, Iska had not detected the presence of another of her kind. Having staked out the outer limits of her range, her path would turn inward, spiraling along an erratic route that wound and twisted its way through the heart of her territory. While doing so, Iska kept the wind in her face at all times; moving into the wind helped ensure her scent and presence would remain unannounced to other animals still out of range of sight and sound. In this fashion, Iska would cover all of her new territory in a week's time or less.

The wolverine quickly climbed its way up a nearby hill to survey the landscape. Although the steep terrain was rugged in the extreme, it didn't significantly slow Iska's progress. Her strong legs and long hooked claws dug into the thin rocky soil creating little puffs of dust and throwing showers of small pebbles in her wake. Before reaching the very top of the hill she stopped - careful not to skyline herself to anything that might be watching the hilltop in the distance. Waiting and sniffing the wind, she cautiously monitored her immediate surroundings. Quietly and patiently, the wolverine remained motionless for several long minutes, refusing to betray her presence - like all wild animals, the wolverine instinctively knew that "movement often killed." Remaining motionless, it flexed its small ears about, listening intently for any sound of trouble or of potential prey. Deciding she was quite alone; Iska crept onward toward the summit. Reaching the highest point, she flattened herself against the earth and took in the lay of the land.

From this point eastward, the tall snowy peaks and jagged crags of the Canadian Rocky Mountain's Eastern Slopes surrendered to Alberta's rounded foothills. To the east, the highlands slowly fell away becoming a series of diminishing hummocks fanning out like ripples within a pond when a stone breaks its surface. Thirty miles further, the foothills disappeared into a sea of prairie grass and sage. These were the Great Western Plains, a geographic feature ranging eastward and lying unbroken for over a thousand miles until reaching the Canadian Shield.

The plains were of no interest to Iska. She was a creature of the high country. Ignoring the lower hills and plains to the east, she turned about, returning in the direction she had come. A new range awaited her, now it was hers to claim.

A Christmas Invitation

Christmas Day arrived bright and clear, the light skiff of last night's snow glistening like diamonds in the morning sun. Harnessing the horse to their buckboard, Grace and Erma began steered the wagon along the snow packed trail toward town. Reaching the recently built town hall, Erma climbed down from the wagon. Taking the reins from her sister, she wound the leather strapping to the hitching post where the wagon sat among others along the hall's frontage. Erma turned intending to assist her very pregnant sister down from the wagon, but discovered a gentleman and his wife had already arrived to lend a hand. The foursome exchanged cheerful holiday greetings while heading toward the hall's open doors.

Approaching the wooden landing, an older man presented himself near the doorway. Dressed in a freshly pressed black suit, shining black cowboy boots, and a white starched collar, the Good Reverend Ronald Hilton welcomed the faithful. The Anglican Church was the first to launch missions at Pincher Creek and other small settlements in the area beginning in February 1889, having first established itself in Fort MacLeod.

Well attended, the service attracted farming and ranching families living within a nearly ten-mile radius. The pastor was a gifted orator, the Good Word and his sermon reaching into the hearts and minds of all present. Erma considered the past several months. While she had been good company for her sister, despite her considerable efforts, the girl knew she was a poor substitute for Grace's husband, George. Nearly two months had passed without a word or message. Erma was relieved when toward the end of the service she glanced toward Grace seeing her sister singing carols and hymns along with the rest of the congregation. In doing so, Erma found her own spirits buoyed by the happy occasion.

Following the service, Erma and Grace drove their wagon toward the general store. Climbing down from the wagon, they placed a feedbag over Red's head and walked toward a largish home to the east of the store belonging to James Schofield. Given Grace's condition and that her husband was off somewhere in the high country with Ned Appleton; Emma Schofield and Lilith Hyde had invited her and Erma to join them at Christmas dinner.

It had been a fine afternoon. Good food, warm conversation, followed by a glass of sherry rounded up the visit. The sun was beginning to drop near the horizon when Grace and Erma thought to return to the farm. James and Emma Schofield followed them out through the front door saying their goodbyes on the porch. James took the opportunity to light his pipe, a habit that Emma forbade within the confines of their home.

As Erma approached Red and removed his feedbag, the horse nuzzled the girl's shoulder anticipating they'd soon leave for home. A whinny sounded a ways up the road and to the west of the wagon, focusing everyone's attention to an approaching sleigh. Obviously one of those travellers the locals referred to as a "mountain men," the long black bearded stranger sat atop a large wooden sled drawn by two heavily shod horses. A beaver hat sat atop his head, thick black shocks of unruly hair poking out from beneath it on every side. With a heavy buffalo coat wrapped about his shoulders and falling well below his knees, Erma saw the rear of the wagon was one large heap of something, the contents hidden beneath a dull brown oilskin tarp; she chuckled to herself thinking the man reminded her of a demented Kris Kringle. Upon reaching Schofield's, the large man removed his hat, grinning broadly and offering a Joyeux Noel to all.

Adrian Bellevue was no stranger to James Schofield. The two had conducted business on numerous occasions since James and Harry Hyde had set up shop in Pincher Creek. Adrian was a rugged individual, one of those few merchants driving cart or sled through the Crows Nest Pass and travelling out to the remote settlements located within British Columbia's Kootenay interior. Prior to James and Harry opening their store in Pincher Creek, Adrian had been obliged to travel the extra forty some miles down to Fort MacLeod to buy his wares before returning westward once again.

Already seated in the wagon beside Erma, the women paused to listen hearing James ask Adrian if he'd heard how the season's trapping was proceeding. Adrian laughed and pointed to the back of the wagon, "What you think?" His Quebecois accent was as thick as his beard.

James removed the pipe stem from his mouth and blew out a small cloud of smoke. "Well, judging from the size of your haul, *plutôt bien jusqu'à présent*. James looked at the women and translated - pretty good so far!" Born and raised in Quebec's Eastern Townships, Schofield spoke Quebecois with ease.

Adrian quickly added. "Oui, bonnes peaux et beaucoup d'entre elles."

Once more, James translated for Grace and her sister; Adrian says good skins and plenty of them.

Grace peppered the two men with a succession of questions. Had Adrian met her husband or heard anything about George Dunn? Ned Appleton? Was the weather good; did you pass Cauldron Mountain?

Her hopes fell when the answers to all her questions proved negative. James saw the woman's disappointed face and sought to improve the situation. "Grace, given the number and quality of the early season's pelts, I'd say it's far more likely than not that George and Ned will return much sooner rather than later. Probably earn a fair profit as well."

On the road home, she and Erma discussed the information furnished by the French trader at some length. Grace had to admit it made sense that a good winter's trapping in one part of the mountain range was likely to be just as good in another. After all, there might be only several hundred miles separating the Kootenays from her husband's trap line. She retired that night praying for her husbands' safe return and that he'd arrive back early in the New Year.

THE TRAP

It was early October and Iska was following her nose which led her along a path that wound through the forests of her new range lying off to the west of Cauldron Mountain. Filtered through the treetops, the rays of the morning sun dappled the forest floor below. Moments before, she had detected the scent and sounds that indicated the presence of prey just ahead; slowing to nearly a crawl, she carefully and silently closed in. Iska pushed her head beneath the branches of a low growing pine discovering a family of fat rodents who were busily gathering the nuts and grasses they would store within their burrow. A full larder would provide the food necessary to survive the approaching winter. Yet, what at first appeared a stroke of good luck, she'd soon discover the fates were stacked against her that day.

A lone male sentry stood alert and erect atop a granite outcropping poking up along the otherwise forested hillside. Compared to his distant cousins living far to the east of the Rockies, the yellow-bellied marmot was truly a giant in every sense of the word. Measuring twenty inches in length and weighing nearly ten pounds, his broad flat head sported a distinctive furry white patch above his dark nose, but he owed his name to the bright yellow fur along his belly and sides. Always attentive and alert to danger, a slight movement in the brush attracted his attention. While unsure of exactly what animal approached, he non-the –less chirped his alarm to the group beyond and within seconds, Iska watched them scuttle into their burrow. The entrance to the underground lair was a small rocky cleft sitting beneath a huge moss and lichen encrusted boulder. The narrow crevice would deny entrance to any animals larger than themselves while the rock surrounding the hole made it impossible for a predator to dig them out.

Nonetheless, Iska wasn't about to give up on the opportunity of a good meal, something she hadn't found in days. She raced to the burrow's entrance and stuck her nose inside; the wonderful aroma of marmot reaching her nostrils increased her hunger. For several minutes, she tore at the rock using her powerful hooked claws without success before checking for an alternate entryway. Moving to the side of the boulder, she scaled the steep earthen slope sniffing for any scent emerging from the ground that might suggest a way to reach her quarry. Luckless, she moved to the boulders opposite side intending to continue her search. That's where she found something she hadn't counted upon.

While working last year's trapline, Ned had spotted a pack of grey wolves near the same boulder. Evidently, the wolves had caught the scent of the hibernating marmots within their burrows. Although a long shot, Ned expertly set and baited a strong steel-jawed trap nearby with the hopes that the wolf pack would return. The wolves had never returned, nor was Ned able to retrieve the trap, a heavy snow combined with his forgetful nature and his failure to adequately mark the traps location left the device unsprung, patiently awaiting whatever might trigger its jaws to close.

One of many "leg hold" trap variations

Iska's sensitive nose gave her no warning of the traps presence; the man's scent had dissipated months before leaving only the autumn leaves and moss to disguise the toothy grey metal. Climbing upward, her front claws only partially gripped the smooth rock causing her to fall back and tumble onto the forest floor. Growling in frustration, she began to rescale the slope once again. Suddenly her ears detected a strange unnatural sound, the click and clack of steel riding atop steel. Stepping down atop the trap's trigger, her weight had released its spring. Instinct led Iska to raise and drawback her paw, but too little avail. The release of the spring's tension sent the trap jumping upwards several inches; the steel jaws closed down upon fur, flesh, and bone. Her front right paw exploded in a blinding moment of white-hot pain.

A CHANGE OF LUCK

New Years Day had arrived a week before. So far, George and Ned had found their efforts handsomely rewarded with an abundance of fine pelts and hides, just as had the owners of those trap lines situated in the Kootenays several hundred miles west as the crow flies. The deer and elk were plentiful and the men ate well, their larder of canned and other foods they'd taken with them, although now diminished, would still see them through for another month or so if necessary. The weather too had cooperated, only a few severe storms and squalls had come their way, and aside from the near constant sub-zero temperatures, the men found day-to-day life quite comfortable. That providence was about to change.

Walking alone, Ned had been on the line for only two out of his normal three-day trek, yet he'd nearly completed his rounds. The trail was hard and easy to walk, only skiffs of light snow had fallen, enough to allow him to see the recent tracks of animals in the area, yet not at all deep. He took whatever animals he found within the traps and snares. Occasionally Ned would reset or move them to locations appearing to possess greater promise.

At one such location, Ned knelt upon the snow carefully resetting a tripped deadfall. The killing stone had somehow become unbalanced, not tripped by an animal, the rock fell to the ground leaving the bait still present and untouched below. A warm quickening breeze passed through the upper boughs of the pines sending a shower of light snow to the ground, some of the flakes reaching Ned's neck found their way into his shirt. He shook his shoulders and ignored the irritation continuing his work. Overhead, the aspen and pines swayed back and forth, their upper branches and limbs creaking like the chorus of a hundred rusty door hinges.

Ned smiled as a warm Chinook wind caressed his rosy cheeks. It had been bitterly cold the past week, but it wouldn't be a short time from now. Warm air gusting eastward from the west coast blew through the low passes of the Rocky Mountain range. The winds were a common and most welcome occurrence in this part of the country. Referred to as "snow eaters" by the aboriginal tribes, the sometimes gale force winds would displace the subzero temperatures at an astounding pace, occasionally raising the ambient temperatures by nearly forty degrees within the space of only several hours.

Ned recalled first hearing of the Chinook winds as a new arrival from Ontario. An old timer he'd met in the streets of Fort MacLeod recalled an occasion when a particularly powerful Chinook arrived; its winds blew in from west traveling due east following the main road through town. Within ten minutes, the center of the road became muddy and bare of snow while the ground closer to its edges was still snow covered and frozen solid. Ned didn't pay the tale much heed until he'd experienced it for himself after moving to Pincher Creek. The town often found itself dead center in the winds passage. The old man may have been exaggerating a might, but he certainly wasn't lying, not by a long shot.

Having newly set the deadfall, Ned walked back to the main trail to where his sled awaited. The wind's speed had increased dramatically, the trunks of the trees growing close to one another began to clap and groan as the wind drove them together and then apart once more. Ned stooped low and reached into a pack atop the sled; a loud crack in the distance drew his attention. He stood up and looked in the direction from which the sound had come. Showers of snow rippled through the forest canopy, here and there dead twigs and small branches rained down onto the earth below, the wind howling like a banshee as it approached. Within a matter of seconds, the sudden powerful gust of wind gripped the trees directly above him; the strength of the blast was such that he felt himself shoved back as if from an invisible hand.

This past summer, the trunk of a long dead aspen had cracked and split during a particularly violent thunderstorm. The still upright twenty-foot section of trunk had come to lean upon the thick limb of a large nearby spruce. Now the Chinook gale blew the trunk free of its precarious mooring causing the dead tree to waver then slowly topple over in slow motion, aimed directly onto Ned's sled that lay on the trail below. Caught up in the surrounding din of the moment, Ned never heard the sound of the widow maker's approach. Moving ever faster during its fall, the thin end of the trunk, still nearly three inches in diameter, struck Ned a glancing blow across his neck and shoulder driving him to the ground. Had the tree fallen only inches further to the right, the deadfall would have squarely struck the man's skull, probably killing Ned instantly.

It took Ned several seconds to figure out what had occurred. Rising to his feet, Ned found himself in a state of shock, shaking and struggling to retain his balance. Meanwhile, a dull throbbing ache slowly grew in his left shoulder - it would take another few minutes before he came to realize the true extent of his injury. The powerful blow had snapped his collarbone and very nearly dislocated his shoulder, its badly sprained ligaments and tendons leaving his left arm nearly useless.

He considered his situation. The tree's heavy trunk lay squarely atop his sled. Given his condition, there was little or no chance of him freeing the sled and dragging it back to the trailhead. Instead, Ned sat atop an exposed corner of the sled for a good twenty minutes. Seeking some physical comfort, he somehow managed to fetch a cigarette from the inside of his coat and struck a match. The tobacco smoke filled his lungs provided him a refreshing rush of normality, at least for the moment. He continued to take stock of his dilemma figuring the trailhead camp still lay nearly six miles distant. If he somehow managed to free the sled, he'd ignore the traps and snares ahead, simply walking along the trail. Doing so Ned figured he had a minimum of four or five painful hours ahead of him. He tossed the cigarette butt into the snow. "Better get at it." he muttered.

Rising to his feet, a knife sharp pain bloomed in his left shoulder. Ned immediately realized there was no way he'd be able to pull the seventy-pound sled, the effort would present too great a challenge. In the end, Ned decided to tighten down the sled's outer tarp as best he could; this would spare it's cargo from the elements and any smaller critters and leaving it where it sat along the trail. Making a sling from a spare shirt, he gently set the damaged limb within its pocket, grimacing from the pain of bending his elbow and redisturbing the injury. He'd take nothing, only the hunting knife and canteen he carried on his belt. Ned gritted his teeth and set off toward the trailhead camp, his rifle firmly gripped in his right hand.

Release

With a pain-filled roar, Iska yanked her right front paw back from the trap. Her powerful teeth bit down scraping across the grey metal that held her fast, but rather than releasing her injured leg, the toothy jaws bit even deeper while still holding fast.

Instinctively, she backed away from the trap dragging it several feet before the chain stretched tight against its anchor buried deep in the frozen soil. Feeling an intense pain running up her entire leg and into her shoulder, she began to panic. This was completely outside Iska's experience. Once again, she bit the steel trap and thrashed violently trying to dislodge the strange creature that held her. Sometime later, realizing she couldn't simply shake herself free, she lay quietly staring at her injured paw. As with so many animals caught in the cruel leg hold traps, Iska had to make a decision, stay and accept whatever fate might await her, or take action, biting and chewing off part of her own paw to escape.

Before the trap had sprung closed, a small branch had fallen between the traps jaws. While its presence hadn't prevented the jaws from tightly gripping two of her toes, the stick had prevented the bones in the paw from breaking. While wrestling with the trap, her paw began to bleed freely, moistening the steel and reducing the friction between her toes and the trap's jaws. A clever and determined animal, Iska would make one final attempt to free herself before carrying out the unthinkable alternative. Steeling herself, Iska braced for the pain the effort would surely bring along with it. Iska pulled back... hard!

Suddenly the pads of her bleeding toes slid past the metal jaws. Her iron hard claws followed a moment later. Growling in both the pain and exhilaration that came with her freedom, she ran from the boulder and into the woods stopping only when she was nearly a quarter mile distant. Her toes would heal in time, but she would never forget or forgive the trap, nor anything, or anyone that might be associated with it.

A BAD BREAK

Ned had arrived at the trailhead an hour after the sun dipped behind the western peaks. The moon would rise later that evening. Until then, the night would remain dark as pitch, lit only by whatever stars might appear, those few shining through a swatch of clear sky. Above camp, a heavy band of cloud formed the classic Chinook arch while in the northern sky, the aurora or northern lights already glowed faintly along the distant horizon.

It had been an arduous hike. He'd made good time the first three miles, but after that, his pace quickly slowed until approaching camp, his progress had slowed to little more than a crawl. Ned's left arm and shoulder throbbed and ached incessantly while the heavy Martini-Henry rifle in his opposite hand seemed to gain weight with every step. Stepping into the small clearing, he quickly looked about for any sign that George might be in camp. The absence of a fire, lit lanterns, and tightly closed tent flaps told him all he needed to know. If George hadn't arrived by now, he was likely spending the night out on the trail. With a deep sigh, Ned prayed silently for George to arrive by tomorrow evening.

Entering his tent, Ned set the long rifle in its usual corner before lighting a candle and setting it on a flat rock positioned beside his bunk. Steeling himself for what would no doubt be a painful effort, he set about lighting the woodstove. Opening its firebox, he thanked himself for having already fed and positioned the kindling before leaving on his rounds. Outside the warm Chinook winds continued to buffet the tent walls sending its tarp flapping and slapping against the canvas, just as they would for the night's duration.

He was ravenous. Fetching a can of salted pork and beans from a wooden footlocker beneath his cot and having but one arm, Ned didn't bother with the can opener, but simply plunged his knife into the top of the can. He worked the wide blade along the can's edges until he could bend the thin metal top back far enough to spoon out the contents. Returning to the locker, he removed a chunk of previously cooked venison wrapped in waxed cheesecloth, wolfing it down in several large bites before gulping mouthfuls of water from his canteen. Seated on his bunk, Ned closed his eyes and struggled with his pain. After about five minutes, the trapper was pleased to find the tent had warmed comfortably.

Rising from the bunk, Ned propped open a tent flap adjusting it until it was little more than a narrow slit. A fresh mountain breeze swept about the tent's interior displacing the stale odor of moldy canvas, old sweat, and wood smoke. He picked up a small kerosene lantern, lifted its glass mantle placing a flame to its wick. After adjusting the flame, he set the lantern down beside the still lit candle atop the flat stone serving as his makeshift night table. Their combined light would allow him to take stock of himself.

Removing the sling, Ned grimaced. Cradling the injured arm as best he could using his right hand, he couldn't help but groan out in pain as he slowly lowered the arm to his waist. Gently removing his coat, a light sweater, and undershirt, he rose to his feet. Approaching a small 4x4 inch silvered metal mirror dangling from the stovepipe; he positioned the lantern using his right hand, adjusting its flickering rays to illuminate his shoulder. Examining his injuries, Ned grew more disappointed and alarmed by the second.

Even given the mirrors poorly defined reflection within the lantern's dim light, Ned easily made out a distinctive pointed bulge jutting upward to the left of his chin. Its presence signalled a broken collarbone, shoulder blade, or both. Spreading atop his shoulder, an angry red black discolouration continued downward, tracing the curve of his chest before pooling within his armpit. Although the injury's initial haemorrhage of broken blood vessels had quelled sometime during his long trek, the blood would continue to drain down until his entire side appeared as one large bruise. No question, it was a bad break requiring attention as soon as possible, but who was there to do it - more over who had the knowledge required to do so? Pincher Creek was the nearest settlement having a proper doctor and that village lay over a hundred miles distant.

Disturbing Discoveries

Straddling a log beside a small cooking fire, George tended its flames in the shelter of a large spruce tree. His Snider Enfield rifle sat propped up to one side - just in case. George munched on a hind leg of a rabbit he'd snared and cleaned the previous day while a can of three-day-old coffee grounds and creek water boiled atop a flat stone set near the flames. Although physically dog tired, his mind continued to work on the troubling situation that made its presence known that morning.

George had approached the simple deadfall, even standing back some distance along the trail he could see its precariously balanced rock had fallen to the ground. Approaching the trap, he assumed that whatever critter had tripped the trap's mechanism now lay crushed beneath the rock. Grabbing an edge, George lifted the chunk of granite to one side and glanced below. Nothing... and the bait was missing as well.

He stood looking about for several long minutes before slowly circling the area, seeking any track or sign that might provide an answer to the puzzle; yet found nothing. Although arriving only that morning, the Chinook had quickly melted away nearly all of the snow cover, leaving the forest floor quite unreadable, moreover, the ground lay scattered with newly fallen twigs and needles. George examined the ground while finding himself suddenly enveloped within a swirling cloud of autumn leaves, their whirling dance orchestrated by the warm winds shifting out of the west. Nature often had an annoying habit of presenting a man with unsolvable mysteries; this one forced George to chalk it up to simple misfortune. With a shake of his head, the trapper reset the deadfall before taking up the reins of his sled and continuing his trek beneath the cool winter sun, the orb appearing pinned and motionless upon the cobalt sky. The Chinook cloudbank that accompanied the weather change had since drifted off far to the south.

Several hours later, George found his original mystery deepening into one of growing concern.

None of his traps, deadfalls, or snares had produced a single "usable" pelt, whatever animal apparently captured. In several of the steel traps, George discovered the partial remains of an ermine and a martin. Their legs remained firmly gripped within the trap's jaws, but something had chewed their bodies free. Continuing onward, he found other deadfalls tripped. Their heavy stones simply brushed aside, the bait consumed.

To George, a bear came to mind as the most likely culprit responsible. Aroused by the warm winds and the scent of food, perhaps the beast awoke from its winter slumber then began following the trapline guided by its nose. George checked the round chambered within his rifle keeping his wits about him. Certainly, whatever was responsible for this mayhem was possessed of some size and power, but an unusual track he discovered within one of the few snow-covered areas still shielded from the sun and wind gave him pause. The track he'd seen was unlike that of a bear, either grizzly or black. The size and depth of the track suggested something smaller, maybe the size of a wolf at best, certainly nothing approaching the weight of even a small bruin.

Most puzzling were the steel traps he'd come across later that afternoon. Some traps were cleverly sprung without effect; their bait lay about uneaten, but not untouched. The trap and bait reeked to high heaven, the musky odor while similar to that of a skunk, remained distinct and unlike anything he'd come across before. Whatever hunger the animal possessed earlier was obviously satiated, the mysterious beast having eaten its fill after dining upon the trapped animals and stolen bait. Yet what of the missing traps?

At several trap sites, George found himself forced to search for his missing equipment at some length. He'd found several that once tripped had been carried off and deposited some fifty to seventy five yards distant from where they'd been placed. A quick inspection of their closed jaws showed the dull metal absent of blood and as clean as a whistle. This was not a case of a trapped animal simply ripping the trap free from its anchorage then having somehow managed to pry itself free of the trap's jaws all without leaving a trace of blood, hair, or fur. No, something was following his trapline; seemingly hell bent upon the destruction of his livelihood.

Leaving the mystery behind at least for the moment, George decided it was time to turn in. He separated what remained of the still burning wood then stirred the ashes about with a stick. A quarter moon peaked through the boughs of a nearby spruce, a small food pouch dangled from a lower branch, out of scent and reach from marauding varmints. Nearby, his bedroll lay bunched atop an oilskin tarp laid across a thick bed of moss gathered to form its base. It made a fine mattress. The night was decidedly warm and pleasant; he needn't shelter beneath the bedroll, but lay atop the tarp. For protection, the long barrelled Enfield lay along one side of his body, his unsheathed hunting knife and hatchet along the other.

The last flames of his fire slowly died, leaving the remaining embers to glow and occasionally spark when a breeze passed above the coals. A small trail of smoke curled upward into the wind then vanished into the dark forest. Some miles distant, a sensitive nose picked up the odor of the burning wood, the unpleasant memory of the recent summer fires resurfaced in Iska's mind. She increased her speed leaving the smoke far behind. A nocturnal animal, her nose and keen eyesight guided her progress as she wandered along George's well-used trail. By the next morning, a large portion of George's trap line lay empty or in ruin, exactly the outcome she intended.

A Good Soaking

The night had proven a long and uncomfortable stretch for Ned Appleton. Dawn arrived finding the man nearly as weary as when he'd first lay upon his cot the evening before. The bone deep ache extended from his shoulder to his waist, although some portion of the pain he felt in his side and back resulted from the precarious poses he'd adopted lying atop his cot while seeking any position that might alleviate his pain. Using his uninjured arm to shift his weight, he painfully rolled his feet off the cot then sat up on its edge. Ned stayed that way for several long minutes, preparing himself to somehow deal with the morning.

Inspecting his left shoulder in the morning light, he found a swollen mass of black and blue flesh and a broken collarbone poking upward at an odd angle. A wave of nausea and fear washed over him. Out here in the wilderness, any injury was dangerous, that danger magnified by the degree of the disability and the distance required to travel for help.

He managed to build a fire then force down a can of bully beef. It was imperative Ned kept up whatever strength he still had. Although tasty, the salty stew invited the diner to wash it down with at least a few large gulps of water. In Ned's case, his injury had caused him to sweat profusely throughout the night. The pain of any movement had overcome his desire to reach his canteen that he'd unthinkingly left out of convenient reach from his cot. Now the lack of water had left him badly dehydrated. He stood up stumbling over to where his canteen hung by its strap and draped over the stub of a nearby branch. Shaking it, he found it nearly empty; he'd have to refill it.

The small pond lay only thirty feet or so distant, but in Ned's condition, it felt like a mile. His feet were leaden and unsteady, his head felt light and his thoughts grew foggy. He arrived at the edge of the water. Gripping the canteen in his right hand, he used his teeth to twist off its cap and then crouched low holding its narrow opening just below the water line. Ned watched the air bubbles exit the rounded neck of the container as the water rushed in to take its place. A moment later, his hand and canteen seemed to rush to the edge of his vision while the pond and forest disappeared into a black void.

Ned's face struck the surface of the icy water and within only moments, the shock revived him, thrusting him back into consciousness. Realizing he'd fallen into the pond, he tried to find his footing in the mud-slicked bottom, but only succeeded in falling backward and further from shore. Instinctively, he flailed with his arms. His right arm rose and fell into the water with a loud splash, but as he attempted to raise the injured arm, the effort resulted in a blinding pain that threatened to thrust him back into unconsciousness.

Only just able to keep his head above the water, he gasped for breath but seemed to take in as much water as air. He choked and by pure chance, his upper body moved forward toward the shore. Sensing he might still save himself, his boots churned and tore at the bottom's sludge. Seconds later and by God's grace, he discovered his feet had somehow found a partial footing. His right hand reached forward grasping hold of the moss-covered bank. His fingers dug deep into the spongy mass. Just below the surface of the moss, Ned felt a network of thin roots belonging to a nearby thicket. Gripping the roots in a vicelike grip, he managed to haul the upper half of his body atop the shore, but the effort had cost him what remained of his strength.

Exhausted and water soaked, he knew hypothermia would soon set in. Already the cold had penetrated his feet, and he could barely feel his legs. He grimaced and managed an ironic chuckle as he realized the icy cold had finally dulled the ache in his shoulder. Ned's eyes closed and as he lay with the heat draining from his body, he mouthed a silent prayer asking that George might somehow return in time to save him, but for the moment, George was miles away dealing with his own set of problems.

Some say the sense of hearing is the last to leave a dying person. Just as Ned passed from consciousness, he imagined he heard a distant whinny and perhaps the clump of a hoof atop the frozen ground.

THE MEETING

Shivering with cold, George awoke beneath a dull grey sky. Rising to his feet, he set about beating his arms against his chest and sides trying to warm himself while looking about. The temperature had quickly fallen in the night and now a brisk north wind signalled a return to winter bringing the smell of snow along with it. He quickly started a small fire and lowered his food pouch from the nearby tree. Finishing off the last of the cold rabbit from last night's dinner, he waited for the coffee to boil. The warmth of the fire and the hot coffee helped to warm him. Thinking back to the night before, he regretted having not crawling beneath his bedroll the night before; George promised himself he wouldn't make that mistake again.

Eager to start out as soon as possible, he quickly organized his equipment then started down the trail toward what he hoped were undisturbed traps and snares. He'd find himself sadly disappointed.

Iska had spent the long hours of the night prowling her territory, her course guided and chosen by her nose and ears. A clever animal and highly adaptive, she quickly learned that following George's trail led to an easy source of food. That night she dined on a Fisher, a mink and several squirrels before amusing herself by tripping the hated steel traps, eating the bait then scattering them about. Just before dawn, she crawled into a high thicket overlooking the last of the deadfalls she'd tripped before drifting off to a light slumber.

George moved down the last section of trail that eventually led toward the trailhead camp. Whatever raided his trapline the day before had been at it again. In various places along the trail, his nose picked up the familiar stink he'd discovered the previous day. Obviously, the other animals in the forest had picked up the scent as well and were determined to steer well clear of whatever it might be, he hadn't caught sight of anything moving. Out of the nearly thirty traps and snares set, two thirds were tripped and empty. The remainder were still set and undisturbed, but none contained an animal of any sort. Moving into the cold breeze, George neared the last of the deadfalls he'd set only half a mile from the trailhead.

Still within her light slumber, Iska's sensitive ears had picked up George's approach from some distance. She raised her head slightly, peering through the thicket's branches and twigs; her ears and eyes focused on a point in the trail where she knew the source of the noise would appear.

Iska had never seen the like of the creature appearing moments later. It walked upright on two legs, the forward positioning of its eyes suggested it was a large predator and unlike any other animal in this forest, its footfall was regular and consistent without pausing to listen for danger. There was little question that whatever it was, it was self assured and therefore very dangerous. More astonishingly was its odd checkered hide, loosely draped about its body, the ragged edges flapped in the wind. She found her eyes drawn to the strange contraption it dragged behind it, what it may or may not be was a total mystery.

Her nose wrinkled and worked to pick up his scent, but she was upwind from the man, the breeze blew her scent toward him likely placing her in danger. She froze in place without moving a muscle; concealment would be her only advantage for now.

George stopped on the trail and removed the light sled harness from his shoulders. The notch he had cut on a nearby tree trunk when first setting his line reminded him of the deadfall's position. Walking a short distance from the trail, he spied the fallen rock signalling the trap lay tripped. Now all that remained was whether an animal lay beneath that rock. He approached the deadfall and lifted the stone; as before, nothing lay beneath, including the bait.

He rose to his feet and stood for several long minutes. Holding his rifle in one hand, George cussed beneath his breath, his eyes glancing about the forest in every direction and seeing nothing out of the ordinary. A moment later, he became aware of a faint yet now familiar smell in the air. Guided by his nose, his head turned northward into the breeze, towards the direction of

Iska's thicket. George's eyes searched the area trying to discern the outline of any animal partially hidden in the brush.

Iska had observed the strange beast as it walked about then approached the deadfall she'd raided near dawn. The angeline was completely amazed that the man hadn't immediately located her sent and position. In fact, he'd even turned his back toward her, something any other animal she'd ever come across would never do. Something was very strange here, and now something else very dangerous had just taken place. She'd followed the creature's eyes, shivering lightly as they came to rest upon her thicket. Fight or flight? Should Iska attack or retreat? Despite the strength and courage she and all her kind possessed, discretion nearly always proved the better choice when it came down to matters of survival.

Making her choice, she bolted from the thicket like a cannon ball from its barrel, swiftly moving upward across the slope and keeping her nose into the wind in a bid to detect other dangers that might lie before her. Within only moments, Iska had loped into the brush moving ever deeper into the forest and towards safety.

The wolverine had caught George completely by surprise as she finally made her move, breaking cover and heading into the trees beyond. The dark furry beast moved with a grace that was almost catlike, jumping and avoiding obstacles with a practiced ease, while at other times simply bulldozing through the dense brush. He'd raised his gun to his shoulder, his finger upon the trigger, but immediately realized the futility of trying a shot. The beast had disappeared; all that remained were the quickly diminishing sounds of cracking twigs and bending branches off in the distance.

He approached the thicket where Iska had been hiding. In what snow remained here and there, he'd found the same odd track he'd seen earlier along the trapline and that same unpleasant musky odor. He'd seen the enemy, now he'd have to figure out a way to defeat it before it cost him the winter's effort.

BACK AT THE FARM

Up to this point, the winter had proven warmer than usual, but now the long expected cold spell may have finally arrived on their doorstep. Stepping out from the warm cottage, Erma exhaled and watched her breath condense into small puffs of haze that rose above her head trailing behind her back as she walked from the cabin. The little clouds reminded her of the steam engine she and her family would watch as it chugged its way into Fort Macleod's railway station. Remembering she hadn't seen her mother, father, and younger sister for almost four months, the young teen suddenly found her previously cheerful mood suddenly growing somber. Feeling small tears forming in the corners of her eyes, she wiped her face with the sleeve of her coat and gave her head a hard shake hoping to dispel the sudden doldrums.

Erma bundled her shawl ever closer about her head and shoulders. Her thin coat draped about the heavy sweater she wore beneath it and the light cotton dress beneath that; yet even so the biting cold soon made its presence known. The girl shivered while unlatching then yanking open the stubborn frost stiffened barn door. Stepping inside Erma immediately noticed a slight rise of temperature within the barn. The body heat of the livestock sheltering within the interior had warmed the barn considerably. After milking their cow, she loosed the horse and cattle into the adjoining corral before collecting a half dozen eggs.

Despite the cold, the large animals obviously enjoyed leaving the barns dim light as they stepped out into the morning's bright sunlight. Red, their old horse, seemed to be feeling his oats and behaving like a yearling colt began chasing the cattle about the corral. Erma watched the action for several minutes then smiled when the old milk cow tired of the game. Simply standing her ground, she lowered her head shaking her horns from side to side. Old Red took the hint and walked away toward a broken hay bale. The horse, cattle, and even the chickens seemed completely unfazed by the subzero temperatures. The girl mused; of course, they had much better coats than hers.

Walking back to the cabin, Erma considered her sister's condition. Grace was growing larger by the day and the expectant mother estimated her due date could be as early as mid-April or as late as mid-May, it was impossible to say. As it was, both she and her sister began to wonder as to the possibility of twins, or God forbid - triplets. In those days a single child, though welcome, was never the less a burden on the family. Food and clothing were less of a concern than the woman's absence from the lighter, but still necessary time-consuming chores; these would come to rest upon her husband.

Multiplying the burden by a factor of two or even three was nearly unthinkable.

Erma arrived at the cabin stomping her feet free of snow on the large flat stones George had set in the earth outside the doorway. When they could afford it George promised his wife, he'd see about putting in a stone or wood-planked floor in the cabin, but for now the dirt floor would have to suffice. Grace smiled as she shouted out, "you'd best not track any of that snow onto my nice clean floor."

Erma stepped into the cabin immediately noting Grace had already completed the day's housekeeping. The cabin's water pails lay refilled from the partially frozen creek. Grace had hauled in a fresh supply of split firewood garnered from a larger pile they stored near the back of the cabin. The recent cold forced the sisters to keep the little wood stove burning hours longer. During the long winter nights, she and Erma would take turns nudging the other awake when it came time to stoke or relight the stove to keep the frost at bay.

The sisters set about taking stock of the cabin's supplies and making a list of what they'd need to buy at Schofields. Grace pulled a small tin can from a wooden box set beneath their bed, dumping coins and a few paper bills across the kitchen table. Counting their meager assets Grace stated, "I only pray George is doing well on his trap line." She shook her head. "Now, if we watch our pennies, we'll be able to make it through the winter, but after that..." She left her sentence unfinished.

SAVIOR

The light snow that had fallen the night before had melted before noon, leaving the trail brown and bare. Before the pair left on their mountain journey, Ned had suggested George mount a pair of small wooden wheels along either rear side of his sled. Doing so would allow the sled to transition into a modified travois when traveling across bare patches of land. By simply shortening up his shoulder harness, the wheeled travois ran atop its wheels behind George allowing him to cross even difficult terrain without too much effort. Easily towing the small wagon behind him along the narrow trail, George was grateful he had taken Ned's advice.

Now nearing late afternoon, George was only a hundred yards or so distant from the trailhead which still lay hidden behind a mixed stand of birch and spruce. Seeing a thin trail of grey smoke of a cooking fire rising above the trees, George looked forward to enjoying Ned's company within the camp. Perhaps Ned could tell him more of the strange creature causing mayhem along his trap line.

Reaching his ears, the whinny of a horse from the direction of the camp caused George to freeze in his tracks. Out in the wilds of the deep woods, a visitor could be exceedingly welcome or exceedingly dangerous. The "long arm of the law" hadn't yet reached these lands. At present, the only applicable law would be the "survival of the fittest." Moving with stealth, George dropped the harness from his shoulders before stepping back and reaching for his Snider-Enfield rifle that lay secured to the travois by a length of rawhide. Freeing the weapon, he brought it to his waist where he cracked opened the rifle breach ensuring a heavy .577 caliber cartridge sat within. Patting his right jacket pocket with his fingers told him an additional four cartridges were available to him should the need arise.

George crept quietly along the trail, keeping as low a profile as possible to minimize his outline while moving among the trees and thickets. Rounding the bend in the trail found George crouched only thirty yards or so from the trailhead camp. Three Indian ponies casually wandered about the camp's outskirts, unfettered and contentedly grazing. A short distance to his right, George saw a young Indian boy standing by the fire poking and adjusting the logs within. On the surface, everything appeared peaceful, but where were the owners of the other two ponies; and where was Ned?

His eyes detected a sudden movement nearby Ned's tent; a moment later, a tent flap opened. The motion seemingly caught the attention of the boy who turned to see what was happening. George's heart raced and his hands shook, but it wasn't from the cold. He was scared and he knew it. Keeping his rifle barrel pointed toward the ground, his hands white knuckled its wooden stock. In his present state, he didn't trust his finger anywhere near the trigger. He watched intently as the flap was lifted clear of the tent entrance. An old man stepped from Ned's tent standing to one side while holding open the canvas flap, shortly two other figures emerged. A large Indian fellow dressed in traditional garb supported Ned as they cleared the tent and walked toward the fire. Even from this distance, George figured his friend looked rather worse for wear.

George stayed hidden while he watched the pair approach and sit at the fire. The young boy removed a pot from beside the fire and poured its steaming contents into a metal mug that he offered to Ned. Ned took it and smiled. George exhaled, his breath rushed from his lungs, he hadn't realized he'd been holding his breath for nearly half a minute. Thanking God for small mercies, he stood up. Holding his rifle to his side, George announced his presence as he walked into camp. All three natives cautiously watched George's approach. Sitting off to Ned's side, the large man searched Ned's face with his eyes before smiling when Ned raised his hand in greeting. Half an hour later, all lay explained.

"I figured I was a goner." Ned said for at least the third time. "If it wasn't for these fellows, I'd have been done in for sure." Ned went on to explain how he came by his injuries and how when he'd gone out to the pond that morning to refill his canteen he'd collapsed into the water. Somehow, he'd managed to crawl out onto the bank, but had soon passed out. Coming to, he discovered himself lying on his bunk covered with blankets while his stove smoked nearby. As hard as he tried, he couldn't remember how he'd come to be there before nearly screaming aloud when old Joseph walked through the tent flap smiling and holding out a mug of birch bark tea, Ned later met Samuel and his young son Jimmy shortly afterward.

Ned took a puff of his cigarette while telling George how Joseph, a tribal Elder and skilled healer had set his collarbone. Still, Ned knew he was in a bad way. The old man didn't speak English so Samuel and Jimmy had taken turns translating for Joseph. "The old man says it looks like the break's a bad one. I can tell you my shoulder and ribs took quite a beating as well." Ned winced as he took a sip of the birch bark tea. "Stuff helps take away some of the pain, but it's as bitter as the north wind. It'll take a might getting used to."

The sun had just set behind the western mountains and the sky was already beginning to darken in the east. Ned poked a stick into the fire with his good hand. It seemed to George that Ned seemed reluctant to say what came next.

"George, I'm afraid I'm done for the rest of the winter. Samuel tells me the old man says I'll be lucky if I can move my arm in a month's time, says it won't regain any real strength until summer." Ned shook his head. "Had to leave my sled out on the trail, figure it's about five miles out."

George waved his hand toward his friend. "Don't worry Ned; I'll fetch it back to camp tomorrow." Continuing he added, "Then we'll go back together, how does that sound?"

"And what, you pulling both sleds? Both fully loaded... I can't see it myself." Ned stared into the fire.

George began to realize he hadn't thought out his offer.

Ned looked George in the face and spoke again. "Listen George, I know you and Grace have need of all the money you can earn this season... for spring planting and all." He paused, George's face acknowledged the truth in Ned's statement. "No, you stay out on your own... it's only a month or so at latest before the season ends. You'll be fine; besides you've learned everything I had to teach you a couple months back. You keep the pelts I left with the sled, they're yours."

Ned glanced to the others present and then back to George. "Sam and his family are headed to a Pow Wow down Cardston way. They've offered to take me along with them and drop me off at the creek. I'll let Grace and the Mounties know where you are."

Knowing Ned's plan made good sense George nodded in agreement. "I guess that's the way it has to be. If Samuel can wait until noon or so, I'll leave early tomorrow morning, drag back your sled and gear. Ned, you'll have some nice pelts to take back, that might make all this worthwhile. "

Samuel spoke up, saying he wouldn't wait any longer than necessary to get on the trail, so in the end, George and Ned decided they would swap sleds, traps and equipment and Ned would leave with Samuel and his group first thing in the morning. Now it was time for a good supper, especially seeing as how George was inheriting the remaining food and canned goods in the trailhead.

Iska's Plan

Iska ran into the wind, darting one way then the other just in case the strange beast was smarter or faster than it looked. After a time, she paused, listening for any sign of her being chased or hunted. Hearing nothing, she satisfied herself the immediate danger had passed. Now it was time for the intensely curious animal to investigate.

The angeline headed southeastward, taking her time and moving with caution as she made a wide circle that would eventually take her downwind of the beast. Approaching the main trail, that George himself had traveled only a few hours earlier, she took up a position atop a small rise affording her a good vantage point. Iska waited for a quarter hour or so before deciding the beast had departed before moving down onto the trail.

Sniffing the ground, she caught the odor of fresh pelts and blood from many animals she was familiar with, most of which she'd fed upon at one time or another. She also picked up the smell of steel and oil, the hated traps Iska had been raising havoc with over the last several days, before traveling north intending to circle back on the beast. Reaching the deadfall she'd tripped the night before she paused. Her curiosity being aroused upon seeing the rock had somehow righted itself above a small portion of meat lying beneath. Still satiated from her raid the night before, she paid no further interest to the bait, instead allowing her nose to focus on the odd scent lying atop the rock and discovered within the depressions in the earth that she correctly reasoned were the beast's footprints. An incredibly intuitive creature, Iska decided the snares and deadfalls also somehow belonged to the beast. As such, the wolverine had a score to settle owing to the creature's intrusion upon her range, the consumption of her prey, as well as the painful attack inflicted upon her by its trap.

Iska knew well the ways of the bear, the wolf, deer, and all the other animals living in the wood. She would observe this new beast from afar, first learning its ways and habits. Once aware of its strengths and weaknesses, she would act. Its trespasses would not lie forgiven or unanswered.

LEGEND

Given the disturbing troubles along his trap line, the unfortunate revelation of his partner's recent disability and meeting Ned's welcome though surprising rescuers, George hadn't given much thought toward food. Now having listened to Ned's account of the matter and feeling at ease, George suddenly couldn't recall ever having been so hungry. An hour had passed; George sat on a stump near a crackling fire almost filled to bursting. Following the meal, Ned once again felt himself becoming fatigued asking Jimmy to help him to his tent. George figured the next day would no doubt prove exhausting and likely very painful for the man. He couldn't blame the man for wanting to wake well rested.

Ned had retired for the night, now George sat by the fire speaking with the others. Beginning his conversation with Samuel, he and George first spoke of what to some might seem nothing more than mere trivialities. The proven questions relating to who, what, when, why, and how? Such small talk was important, quickly discerning a person's values and beliefs yet by not only what they said, but also how they said it, and the ease with which the conversation flowed. So unlike the present day, where chosen words and phrases work to shield our inner most thoughts and personalities, our conversations carefully gauged, measured, and couched within accepted political and social jargon.

Earlier that fall, Samuel and his son Jimmy had agreed to accompany the old man on a special vision quest. The small group traveled out to a distant cave the Elder remembered from his youth, many years past. The old man knew his time was coming and sought to reconnect with the spirits before passing over into their world.

Vision quests were a rite of passage for the young men of many indigenous nations. Typically, an older tribesman would accompany the youth to an isolated location. Upon arrival, the older man would remain at distance, ensuring the youth's safety while the boy underwent his quest. Forgoing food and drink for several days, the boy would engage in prayer or ritual. During this time, a specific animal might announce itself to a virtuous traveler functioning as the young brave's "spirit guide," and leading the youth into an ethereal journey or realistic dreamscape. Once completed, the youth would return home to seek help and advice from the village's elders, shamans, or medicine men to interpret the experience.

Joseph had visited the same cave with his father as a young man, just as his father had done so in the company of Joseph's grandfather. The old man had waited one summer too many to repeat the journey on his own and believing he wouldn't live another year asked for Samuel's help. Given the Elder's stature within the tribe, Samuel had quickly acceded to the request; it was both an obligation and an honor. Besides, Jimmy would reach the age of passage the following year; knowing the cave's location and its powerful connection to the spiritual realm might aid his son in his own vision quest.

Eventually the talk turned to hunting then quickly moved on to trapping. The Indian tribes were well versed in the nature of deadfalls and snares having done so for centuries before the arrival of the whites and their steel traps. Asked whether the season had been as favorable to George as it had been to Ned, George explained the recent troubles along his trap line then described the strange animal he'd seen only that morning. The conversation abruptly ceased and the night became still as death.

Samuel and Jimmy looked to one another before each turned toward the old man. Joseph studied the troubling expressions painted on the faces of the younger men as Samuel quietly spoke a single word - Kuekuatsheu. The old man nodded toward the men placing several questions to Samuel in the language of the Cree nation while Jimmy added several small branches then a heavier chunk of firewood atop the fire. As the fresh wood made contact with the fire's white-hot embers, the flames blazed upward, almost as if someone tossed a can of kerosene upon the flames.

The old man's eyes turned away from Samuel, his gaze locking onto George's questioning eyes. Joseph spoke slowly and with considerable deliberation then waited for Samuel to translate. Maybe it was the Elder's expression, his almost reverent tone, or simply the cold of the night, but either way George felt a chill run up his back as Samuel rendered the Elder's words back to him in English.

"Kwekwatshew. " Samuel carefully pronounced the name of an old nemesis known to all Indian peoples - "Kway-kwah-choo, the "Evil One." Hearing those words, Jimmy ceased administering to the fire and sat quietly atop a log listening attentively.

"The creature is possessed by the spirit of an evil shaman, with the strength of a demon from before the beginning of the world. Some legends say it was the Kwekwatshew that helped create the world." The old man's eyes closed lightly trying to recall a distant memory then began again to speak.

"The "Evil One" arrives in the depths of winter. Both night and day it seeks the trail of a man. Once found the creature follows it, never losing scent or sign. If the trail leads over a windswept frozen lake and the hunter's footprints become unseen, it will follow the shoreline for miles until it again crosses the man's track leading back into the forest. It visits the traps and snares of the hunter's trap walk. It destroys the traps, drags out the captured animal mauling and ripping it to pieces before hiding it in the underbrush or even atop a high pine. The fiend rarely eats much of any animal; its true interest lies in destruction and the feeding of its hunger for everything wicked. Once the Kwekwatshew has found the trapping-walk, the hunter has no choice but to abandon the area and travel some distance before building new traps. If he is very lucky the hunter may take new furs before the evil one discovers his new trap walk." The Elder paused.

Growing silent, the Elder lifted his head and looked up into the sky. The aurora weaved intricate curtains of green, blue and red that randomly faded and brightened anew. "The dance of the dead men" he stated solemnly.

After listening carefully, George spoke up. "What can be done to stop it?" He immediately corrected himself. "How do I kill it?"

Samuel looked at the old man who now stared into the campfire's flames; he was lost in thought. "The Elder can tell you nothing more." Samuel looked into George's eyes. "But I can."

George heard Ned coughing and groaning within his tent. Jimmy got up off his log and walked over to check on the injured man.

Samuel continued. "What the Elder has told you is true. The legends of the past do not lie of the creature's cleverness and strength. Even so, a man may kill or trap a Kwekwatshew. Two winters past, I met a white trapper in the Kootenays. We shared a fire and he showed me the skin of a Kwekwatshew he had trapped and killed."

"Did he use steel traps?" George asked.

Samuel shook his head. "No. The trapper told me the demon tripped all his steel traps, many of them were carried off and lost." Samuel paused. "He used a box. Do you know of such a thing?" George shook his head, the Indian continued.

"The trap works because the Kwekwatshew is very curious. The hunter started by building a box of strong logs, about this big." Samuel pressed the fingers and thumbs of each hand together forming a rough circle perhaps four or five inches in diameter. "They cannot be smaller; the claws of the demon will rip them apart."

George anticipated the trap's design in his mind. "So bait is placed inside and the hunter left a hole so the wolverine could climb inside?"

"Yes, in a way." Samuel's answer was curt. He waited a moment before explaining further.

"The top and sides of the box are enclosed, but for a single opening positioned near the upper edge, along one side of the box. This opening he covered with small thin branches; this is where the demon will enter. The trapper knew that had he left the opening clear, Kwekwatshew would expect a trick and the trap would not work." Samuel went on to explain that the wolverine would work at the sides and roof of the box testing their strength until it located the weak entrance and tore it open. Before sealing the box, the trapper had hung a chunk of meat from the ceiling, held by a weak slender cord. Directly beneath the bait the hunter had buried sharpened stakes within the earth, their spear-like edges pointing upward toward the bait he had suspended above. The wolverine would balance itself within the opening, pawing at the bait and trying to bring it towards him, but the hunter being smarter, had tied it out of easy reach. Becoming frustrated, the wolverine leapt onto the hanging meat, the thin cord snapped beneath its weight, and the wolverine fell and died on the sharp stakes below."

Neither man said a word for nearly a minute before George broke the silence. "This is the only way to trap the demon?"

"Yes. I know of no other." Samuel spoke with confidence, but then lowered his voice. "It is still a much better idea that you move on. There are risks in doing battle with the demon. Kwekwatshew is clever, strong, and wicked. He will kill you if he is able."

George sat by the fire, his attention drawn to Jimmy who was walking back from Ned's tent. "Father, the white man is in pain and cannot sleep. He asks that the Elder make some more birch bark tea." Seeming to know what Ned requested Joseph already had moved toward the blackened pot sitting near the fire. Fetching a small handful of bark shavings along with several other healing herbs he carried in a pouch at his side, he dropped the combination into the near boiling water.

The wind suddenly shifted direction, now coming out of the north. George and Samuel looked up to the starry night sky and found it quickly becoming obscured; one by one the glistening diamonds of light were hidden behind the vague edges of a dark cloud - sometime later tonight it would snow.

It would prove a long and difficult night for Ned, but in the morning the Elder's ministering seemed to have helped greatly. George securely bound his swapped pelts atop Ned's travois. The rest of his equipment was loaded on his sled and tied to Ned's sling. The sun had been up for less than an hour when Samuel signalled the small group of travellers to begin their eastward trek along the base of Cauldron Mountain.

Ned waved to his friend and yelled out. "Don't worry George! I'll tell Grace I left you in good health and spirits!" George watched the travois bump along the snowy trail until it entered the woods and moved from his sight.

George spoke softly. "God speed Ned. God speed."

Temporary Respites

George retraced Ned's steps along his trapline as they led away from the trailhead camp. He finally came across his friend's abandoned sled near noon. The day had remained cold and dull. Low grey clouds drifted across the sky occasionally bringing with them short squalls of snow. George examined the scene before him. As far as the sled's condition, everything seemed to be in once piece, the equipment and pelts still lay bound securely to the sled's undamaged frame.

George had to struggle to lift the dead weight from atop the sled in order to free it. As it fell, the heavy branch had only glanced Ned's neck and shoulder, despite being badly injured, it was quite apparent that Ned was a lucky man, had the branch struck his friend's skull, George figured Ned would very probably have been killed in an instant.

George arrived back at the trailhead camp without incident or difficulty. He spent the remainder of the day taking inventory of his equipment and supplies. Taking Ned's pelts off the sled, he added these to a tarped bundle of his own that hung from a strong branch and suspended using a length of hemp. This prevented animals from getting at the pelts.

On a more important note, hanging beneath another tree branch a good distance from his tent and wrapped in similar fashion were George's perishables. Composed of salted meat, fish, or game, these items were stored well away from the sleeping quarters. This was quite unlike the canned goods that had little or no scent and could safely remain within the tent. Although bears were most likely asleep in their dens, from time to time they did arouse and roam about, especially when the weather was favorable. Keeping food in your tent with a hungry bear in the vicinity was a recipe for disaster, especially if you happened to be within the tent when he came by for a visit.

Early the next morning, George set off to check Ned's trap line. He felt there was little sense checking his own line since he figured the wolverine had already done its worst. He only hoped to discover Ned's line had fared better than his own. By the end of the first day, the outlook appeared favorable; he'd taken no fewer than nine fine pelts from Ned's marked snares and traps. Better than that, George hadn't found any indication that the wolverine had made any appearance whatsoever. He considered the situation; perhaps the beast had just been passing through when it happened upon his trap line before moving on; maybe the old man's frightening story was merely that, a story. Perhaps he'd return to his line and discover it undamaged as well?

Iska would quickly prove just how very wrong George's assumption was.

Iska's Decision

The range to which Iska had laid claim was huge, even for one of her nomadic tribe. It would take the angeline the better part of fifteen days to circuit its outer boundaries, and yet as many again to patrol its interior. Sadly for George and Ned, their trap lines happened to lie within the boundaries of her range. Days before, she had backtracked and reconnoitred George's original trapline, but unable to find any trace of the man, she paid the intrusion no further mind and once again set about her routine patrol. In past months, Iska had come across Ned's scent on two occasions, but the trail was nearly a week old and the scent was barely detectable. As long as the intruder didn't plan to stay, she hadn't known or cared what sort of creature might have passed through.

This situation changed but a day earlier when Iska chanced upon the location where the falling tree had struck Ned days before. The bands of light snow moving through the land hadn't hidden his footprints along the well-worn trail, yet it hardly mattered; she needed only her nose to provide the information she required. During George's visit only a day earlier, he had deposited his fresh scent upon the fallen log he'd lifted from the sled. The renewed presence of her enemy provided her the determination to follow his trail, discover whatever mischief he might be up to, and then drive the beast from her realm by whatever means necessary once and for all.

A Sneak Attack

George had left the trailhead camp two days earlier. He'd be absent for several more as he worked to combine each of the more productive sections of both trap lines into a single manageable circuit. He took care to remark the location of the traps, snares, and deadfalls while moving along the trail; failing to do so; a heavy snowfall could easily hide their location. If there was a single thing George learned this winter, it was that the forest constantly changed its appearance with the ease of a woman slipping on a new dress.

George felt renewed and excited about the trap line he was laying down. The weather couldn't have been more perfect, the light snowfalls over the last few days created a blank slate upon which many fur bearing animals had left their mark. At this point in the season, George could easily read the track and signs of nearly all the animals living in the forest and had set his traps accordingly. When he returned in three days time, he expected he would discover a fine bounty, but for now, he pressed on with his work.

Iska easily followed George's tracks arriving at the trailhead camp early the next morning. Cautiously exploring the vacant camp's perimeter with her nose and ears, she found the camp silent but for the occasional chatter of a curious squirrel who'd noticed her intrusion and a pair of Canada Jays that floated like grey ghosts about the site while searching for morsels of food. Within the camp itself, the fresh snow cover lay unbroken upon the ground. She ventured closer, picking up the faint scent of horse mingled with those of various men. Arriving at George's tent, she discovered the malodorous stink of her enemy to be strongest here - this must be his den. Iska circled the tent then forced her head beneath a lower tent flap preparing to enter and explore within, but the presence of another odor restrained her from doing so. Over the season, the smoke from the small stove within had permeated the interior canvas and bedding. The vivid memory of the previous forest fire and its flames were still too fresh in her mind, refusing her direct entry.

Iska contented herself in using her strong sharp claws to rip wide gashes along the sides of the tent and reducing the canvas to little more than shreds before moving on to destroy anything that lay beyond. It didn't take her long to discover the food cache George had hung from a high spruce branch near the edge of camp. She climbed the tree with ease then gnawed through the rope causing the sack to fall upon the earth. Now having descended from the tree, she set about ripping and tearing open the cache. A feast of frozen venison was Iska's reward. After eating a sizable portion, she sprayed the remaining meat with her oily pungent scent before scattering the polluted food about the base of the tree.

It took her slightly longer to discover George's pelts. The oil tarp had disguised the hide's odors, but eventually she discovered the large bundle hanging down from a tree limb. Once again, she climbed and gnawed through the thick hemp rope, watching the bundle tumble to the snow below. Climbing down Iska systematically tore through the tarp exposing the season's pelts. One by one, she pulled the hides from the tarp ripping and tearing each into pieces. Completing the mauling the pelts, she urinated on some of the scraps, before marking the others with her reek.

Her work done she walked the camps perimeter until she discovered what she sought. That point at which George's most recent track re-entered the forest and where his new trap line began.

A Winter's Dream

Following a disquieting nightmare, Grace had experienced a fitful restless night. Unable to return to sleep, she tossed and turned upon the thin mattress, wrapping her nightgown tightly about her growing tummy while twisting her legs and feet among the sheets beneath the heavy comforter. Despite all attempts to the contrary, Grace's mind returned to wander the worrisome dreamscape time and again.

Ten minutes earlier Grace's hand had groped across the night table beside the bed. Finding what she sought beneath her fingers, she closed her hand feeling the reassuring wooden beads of her rosary. She wrestled with her thoughts and tried to alleviate her fears while holding the rosary close to her breast to pray. Upon previous nights, prayer had calmed her fears and worries for her man, but tonight was different. Now, in these anxious moments and with a late winter's dawn still hours away, she sensed George was at risk from another peril other than merely the elements, the steep rugged terrain, or the accidental misfortunes these and other dangers his venture might encompass. This new threat was quite different, as if directed toward the man with a singular malice and purpose.

Lying beside her pregnant sister, Erma endured the nocturnal ballet with considerable but waning patience. On her right, she felt the mattress depress as Grace sat up on the side of the bed obviously surrendering any hope of returning to sleep. Erma, herself now fully awake, tilted her head back on her pillow, looking toward the small window. A late crescent moon floated within its warped glass pane, she tried to gauge the time of night and the day's sunrise. The girl lifted her head from the mattress then supported her head on her elbow, her eyes following her sister as she rose from the bed and slipped on her leather shoes. The room was nearly as black as sackcloth. If it were not for the weak glow of the few smoldering coals and embers that refused to die within the stove's firebox, Erma would have been unable to trace the outline of her sister's flowing nightgown as she moved about the room.

Several minutes later, Erma shook her head then threw her own feet across the bed. "Well, I might as well join you. You could at least light a candle while I go outside for a pee." Leaving the cabin door, she heard her sister sobbing quietly in the dark behind her.

Minutes later, Erma re-entered the cabin. Her sister sat at the table her worried features candle lit, Erma could see the glistening tears her sister continued to dab away with a small hanky. Pretending not to notice, Erma went about adding wood to the fire, filling the kettle and loading the teapot. While waiting for the kettle the girl busied herself, brushing her hair and thinking about the day that lay ahead. Hearing the kettle's whistle, Erma lifted it from the stove and filled the teapot, setting it and several mugs atop the table before taking a chair across from Grace.

Erma looked into her sister's face watching Grace shake away the last of the doldrums and regain control. Supported by the presence of her sister and the candle light, Grace searched for the words to describe the terrors invading her mind earlier in the night. They came slowly.

"Erma; I saw George. He was out there in the woods ... and Ned wasn't there. Just George, he was all alone." With the recollection of her dream, her emotions welled up and she placed a hand upon her belly feeling the baby stir within.

"Grace, it was just a dream." Erma reached across the table and took her sisters hand. "George and Ned are well, they'll be back soon; remember what the trapper said at Schofield's last week?" She and Grace had arrived at the store to find a saddle horse and a fully loaded pack mule tied up at the hitching post. Going inside, they listened to a bearded grizzled man speaking with Harry Hyde. The man had been trapping down south, near Waterton village. The season had treated him so well he'd been able to shut down his line, now he was on his way to Fort Macleod to sell his furs.

"Yes, I know you're right. But this... this dream was just so real." Grace paused then grasped her sister's outstretched hand within both of hers. "Oh Erma! There is something out there with George. Something..." Grace knew she would sound melodramatic, but carried on anyway. "Something evil, something out there means to do George harm. I don't know how I know it, I just do!"

The women carried on speaking throughout the predawn hours. Grace sought to explain the certain knowledge that her husband was in danger. "Call it woman's intuition, or maybe my being with child has something to do with my feelings." she offered. "Do you remember, Sophia?"

Erma was too young to remember her aunt's strange predictive abilities while pregnant, but she'd heard her mother, friends and relatives recollect those occasions often enough. Sophia had calmly predicted the very moment when someone's husband had lain crushed beneath a supporting timber in the company mine. The wooden timber had cracked and shattered, sending nearly a ton of rock and ore tumbling down atop several men. On another occasion, she'd correctly foretold a distant uncle's departure from this earth going so far as to cite the particular date and even the hour - a letter arrived nearly a month later informing the family of his death and confirming the very same details Sophia had spoken of. Yet more often, it was little more Sophia's sharing her vague feeling that a friend could be expected for tea; something quietly dismissed when failing, but quickly celebrated at length when proven correct.

Grace hoped the frightening dream was nothing more than her missing George and anticipating their child's arrival. The first rays of the morning sun quickly dispelled the night's discomforting thoughts and lingering emotions.

A Shattering Discovery

George arrived to find his tent in ragged ruins, his entire food cache and at least half the season's pelts destroyed. While surveying and repairing what damage he could, his mind replayed the conversation with Samuel and Joseph the night prior to Ned and the others departed the trailhead camp.

"The Evil One arrived in winter seeking the trail of a man. It follows the hunter's track visiting the traps and snares along the hunter's trap walk. It destroys everything it can find, it's only interest is in destruction and feeding its thirst for everything wicked. A wise hunter will quickly abandon the trap line at times travelling a good distance before taking the chance to set new traps - although the evil one will eventually rediscover the new trap line."

George packed his gear and supplies piling them upon the remaining sled. While doing so, he mused over the possibility of moving on to another area he and Ned thought promising enough to try out next season. It was always a good idea to leave an area at rest and untapped for several years before returning. By the time he'd finished loading the sled, he'd decided to retrace his steps and head east along the Cauldron pass then continue south for several miles, following the high country along the eastern slopes. Once arriving, he'd set up a small base camp before setting out a new trapline. Although it was nearly the second week of February, with any luck, he'd return with enough pelts to see him and Grace manage both spring planting and holding on through the summer until the fall harvest.

But luck is a fickle mistress, and there were many possibilities. Would the weather hold? Would the rugged lands permit him entry? Would the animals be plentiful and of course most pressing; would the wolverine continue to follow and hound his every step? George would just have to do what he could to even the odds. As he left the trailhead and headed up the Cauldron Pass, George's mind worked on the design of the trap Samuel had described to him. He also had another idea he'd employ to defeat his nemesis. An ambush he had devised would require both patience and fortitude in addition to a keen eye and a steady hand. Suddenly he had a feeling of confidence that one or the other of his plans would certainly work; they simply had too!

Iska's Decision

Since the summer fires and her initial contact with man and his traps, a slow change had taken place within the animal's psyche. With each trap, snare and deadfall she discovered and destroyed; a strange satisfaction seized hold of her. Aside from an adult grizzly bear or a larger wolverine, Iska considered herself the queen of whatever part of the forest she walked. For a time, her confidence remained badly shaken since that first brief encounter on the trapline when she had chosen to flee rather than engage with the strange beast. This all changed when she came upon the trailhead campsite - whatever these animals might be, they were no more than that. They used dens, they cached food, but most importantly, they hunted prey within her range!

Within Iska's complex mind, she remembered the destruction of the camp several days earlier with a grim satisfaction. Now revisiting the camp and discovering the man had abandoned the site, she felt her sense of dominion proved beyond any doubt. Now it was time to drive the man from her range and make sure neither he nor any other of his kind ever trespass again.

With a snarl and a low growl in her throat, she set out toward the Cauldron Pass following George's passage into the alpine forest. Now it was his turn to flee, and she'd best not catch up with him.

Setting the Trap

George wouldn't take the time to rebuild a full camp; it was late in the season. He was better off spending more of his time setting up and running the new trap line. However, in the meantime he had something more important to attend to - a trap. Before constructing the trap's design as described by Samuel, George had to consider several factors regarding its placement.

Moving easily during the hours of darkness, the wolverine relied on its sensitive nose, ears and unusually keen night vision. If the animal doesn't hear or sense movement in the area, its path will constantly amble along the terrain hoping to pick up the scent of its prey from tracks on the ground, but preferably atop the wind. Once detected, the predator will approach, constantly moving upwind, keeping the other animal's scent within its nostrils while its own scent drifts downwind and away from its prey.

The second factor considered was the movement of local air currents. Like most hunters, George knew that during the daylight hours, as the air gradually warmed within the vales and ravines, it moved upslope taking with it the scent of any creature below. The opposite situation occurred at night when cooler air descended from the upper slopes collecting within the valley. In either case, an animal's scent rode upon a breeze that might betray its presence at any moment.

George would locate the trap within a broad U-shaped ravine lying below the northwest ridgeline, an area both sparsely wooded and clear of dense brush and the larger trees in the forest. The absence of heavy trees and brush, as well as the snowy surface of the river provided George a number of clear shooting lanes. A small river passed through the ravine and in some places, the water bubbled and gurgled above the river's surface that was still thinly ice and snow covered this late in the season. George reasoned the location was ideal for his purposes.

Since the wolverine was most active during the hours of darkness, the night breezes would likely carry the odor of the trap's bait with them as they flowed up the shallow side of the ridge and fanned off to the northwest. With any luck, the wolverine's wide meanderings would see it come across the foul, yet appealing stink of the half-rotten bait. Once picking up the trail, the animal should approach the trap from the north, George planned to wait to the south of the trap, his own scent masked by that of a skunk he'd found in his trap several days earlier. The presence of natural background noise, in this case, the bubbling river water, would help disguise any slight sounds he might make while lying in wait.

Given the animal comfortably hunted and moved about in near total darkness, it was truly fortunate that the bright gibbous or nearly full moon rose early in the evening and stayed high in the sky throughout the night. The moonlight would work in his favor, reflected off the river's snowy surface it would illuminate the trap and the surrounding area. Feeling the circumstances and the wind direction were about as good as they were likely to get, George baited the trap then took up a well-concealed position behind a bough enclosed blind and within easy range of his rifle. George felt confident that should the trap not succeed, his Enfield rifle most certainly would.

FOLLOWING HER NOSE

Over the past several days, Iska had little problem following George's trail. Instead of winding through aspen forest and grassy lowlands, the easily walkable trail along the Cauldron Pass cut nearly due east. Along its lower sections, the pass's southern border was lined with stands of thick buck brush, while higher up, the jack pines grew as thick and close as the bars of a prison cell and nearly impenetrable to either man or beast. The northern slopes weren't any better. Here the trees were predominantly black spruce, and though widely spaced, the forest floor lay carpeted in deep banks of feathered moss. Growing up to several feet thick, the deceptive banks of moss disguised a treacherous landscape full of broken rock, rotting logs, and shallow pits; one wrong step might mean a bad sprain, a broken leg or even worse.

Iska reached the pass's summit. She had visited here once before while setting the borders of her eastern range. From this point, the Eastern slopes of the Rocky Mountains ran north and south, while to the east those peaks vanished, the topography morphing into succeeding waves of wooded foothills, each series lower than its predecessor until at last becoming a vast plain.

That night she followed his trail across a high, tree barren ridge that stretched off to the south before dropping down into a dry gravelled wash. The wash ran for several miles before the terrain became very similar to that where Ned and George had chosen to set up their first trap lines. Moving through the countryside, her nose and keen ears picked up the scent of many prey animals and predators. While she was quite able to kill enough small game to ensure her survival, she much preferred being the first to discover the carrion of larger animals such as deer, elk, or moose. Once found, she would spray urine and her strong musty scent about the kill site serving to warn off other predators while making the meat itself quite unpalatable to their taste.

She renewed her travels along the eastern slopes early the next evening following George's freshly laid and easily followed trail. Everything was going in her favor until she came upon a long stretch of open river. George had chanced crossing the ice thin surface of the river only a day earlier. During that crossing, a foot or sled runner had occasionally broken through the rotten ice threatening to send him into the river and drown him within its deep waters and strong current. Upon reaching the opposite side, George chided himself for taking such a reckless path swearing he'd never repeat that mistake again.

Iska stood on the riverbank looking southward across the water. Iska could swim, but she wouldn't take the chance crossing a fast flowing, ice choked river. Should an animal suffer a significant injury, its chances of survival dropped at a frightening rate. No animal living in the wilderness would make the crossing unless it had no other option. Instead, Iska chose to move west, traveling upslope, she made her way along the river's northern bank. She'd lose time until she could either ford the river where it grew shallow or cross at a point where the early spring ice still lay intact. There was little choice if she were to continue her quest. Once safely across, the angeline would press east along the opposite bank until she came across his trail once again.

Springing the Trap

For the second night, George again sat on a large stump, his body well concealed within the blind. He rubbed his tired eyes. Over the last several hours, his eyes lay fixed on the trap lying some two hundred yards distant. His rifle loaded and at the ready, it rested on several stacked logs lying before him, this makeshift platform would afford him a rough though adequate shooting bench. The additional stability would help him target the wolverine if by some remote chance it managed to avoid the pit and the razor sharp, embedded stakes driven into the near frozen earth below. Another hunter might have positioned his blind some hundred yards or so further back from the trap, but George doubted his ability to make the shot, especially at night.

In the valley, the night air was cool and nearly still. George licked a finger and held it up into the air to gauge the direction of any breeze that might be present. He smiled, he and his blind were presently downwind of the trap. Now all he could hope for was that the wolverine would have already picked up the scent of the bait while avoiding his own.

He took a swig of water from his canteen then set it by his feet before continuing his vigil. He peered between the freshly cut spruce boughs positioned on and in front of a checkered framework of larger branches he'd fashioned several days earlier. The moon was nearly full, its brilliance spilled across the valley bathing everything it touched within a silvery light. The stark contrast between light and shadow was as sharp as a knife-edge. The tree's trunks and branches cast strange snaking figures upon the snow-covered ground. Waiting so patiently and still, at times George almost imagined he could see those shadows creeping along the earth together with the moon's unhurried passage. Every so often a wispy bank of high cirrus cloud would drift across the moon's face, bringing with it subtle changes to the surroundings. Considering its position in the sky, George roughly judged it might be approaching midnight.

The wolverine was little more than a silent black ghost in the night. Its footfall remained both light and quick as it ran atop the longer logs lying on the forest floor or skipped over smaller branches and dried twigs. All the while, the creature somehow managed to avoid making a single crack or even a slight rustle in the underbrush. Every so often, the creature would grasp the rough gnarled bark of a large spruce or fir, then using its powerful claws and legs would propel itself up the trunk until reaching a point allowing it to survey the terrain below.

The wolverine had been patrolling its range along the high upper ridge, somewhere northwest of the trap. Nearing the edge of the high tree line, its nose detected the faint aroma of mouldering meat rising upon the warmer air from the valley floor still a good distance below. Enticed by the odor, the wolverine descended into the valley, its course meandering first one way and then another, all the while drawn forward by the promise of an easy meal, the beast continued tracing the scent back to its source. Now that sensitive nose told it a meal was close at hand.

George was almost ready to call it a night. He'd been sitting in one place since shortly after dark. Now hours later his butt had fallen asleep, his knees had stiffened and his entire body was demanding a good stretch. He was shifting his weight preparing to stand when he detected a movement on the hillside somewhere just above the trap. His aching body immediately forgotten, he resumed his previous position scanning the area before him. Five long minutes passed without him perceiving any further motion. George began to think he'd been seeing things until a large dark shape moved rapidly across the ground. It paused shortly at the trap's log base before rounding the trap, sniffing, and snuffling as it moved along. There was no question in George's mind as to what it might be... the wolverine! The black outline disappeared behind the trap for several minutes. When it reappeared, it had crept atop the trap's roof obviously searching for an easy entrance, seconds later it discovered the slender branches and thin twigs disguising the trap's entrance.

A Great Horned owl perching directly above George's blind hooted loudly several times before spreading its wings and lifting off its branch. George had just about crapped himself right then and there, but thankfully he'd been too startled to even move a muscle! He watched the large bird glide over the river with a noiseless grace. Within a matter of seconds, the owl disappeared within a stand of leaf bare birch and aspen.

No longer distracted, he looked back to the trap... the wolverine had disappeared. For nearly five minutes, George waited in silent agony; his muscles taught and aching, his ears and eyes straining with effort while his mind did its best to conjure and tease any image at all from the dark forest... his patience was soon rewarded.

George stared as the wolverine reappeared; it now clung effortlessly to the thick logs forming the side of the trap. Its head drew near the opening and paused obviously sniffing about. A moment later, a set of powerful claws tore away the small twigs covering the entrance, cleared of the obstruction; George watched the wolverine poke its head within the entrance. A second later, the animal retracted its head then spent a full minute looking about and searching for any sound or movement that might betray the location of a potential enemy.

George had been expecting the wolverine to enter the trap in a slow and cautious manner, but that wasn't in the animal's nature. It disappeared from George's view in a flash. Entering the trap, the wolverine had leapt atop the hanging chunk of rotting venison. For a short moment, both its body and the bait swayed back and forth, but only for a matter of seconds. The combination of its weight and that of the venison were too much for the intentionally flimsy piece of hemp George had purposefully fashioned to hang the bait.

In what had moments before been absolute silence, George now heard rather that saw the animal as it dived through the entranceway to seize the suspended bait. The thin rope groaned with the additional sudden weight then snapped, sending the animal tumbling downward where it impaled itself upon the razor sharp stakes. A series of eerie screams and howls erupted and echoed from the trap's black interior. George sat petrified; the crashing din seemed to go on forever before the cries softened, finally reduced to only an occasional mew or soft growl. He waited an eternity before chancing any movement.

Finally, when George couldn't bare the suspense any longer, he stood up from behind the blind stretching his back and legs. Grabbing his rifle, he began a slow walk on unsteady legs crossing the uneven forest floor and making his way to the trap, all the while keeping his eyes keen and his ears pricked for any evidence that the creature still might live. Reaching the trap he raised and pointed the barrel of the rifle toward the opening then kicked the bottom logs several times with his boot... nothing, not a sound. George repeated the action several more times until satisfying himself the wolverine probably lay dead within, but there was no way he was going to stick his head in there tonight to make sure of it. No, he'd leave the job of ripping apart the trap until the light of morning.

Dead tired, yet feeling triumphant, George returned to his leanto, throwing himself atop the bedroll and pulling the oilskin tarp across his body. Moments later, he was in a deep sleep and wouldn't stir until well after sunrise.

An Arrival in Pincher Creek

Erma was dusting the top shelves in Schofield's when she heard the small bell hanging above the store's front door tinkle shortly before drowned beneath the harsh creaks of the front door's rusting hinges. She heard James Schofield's voice call out from the back room while she turned her head toward the doorway. A young Indian boy Erma didn't recognize stood in the open doorway then quickly moved aside while continuing to hold the door open.

"Be right there." James announced and moments later strode into the store wearing one of his wife's aprons. Quickly realizing what he must look like he stripped the apron from his person. "Er, just doing a bit of spring cleaning... might dusty back there." He chuckled to himself and held the apron in his hands watching three men squeeze through the tight doorway. Two of the men supported a third between them.

Recognizing whom it was that they carried, Schofield blurted out in surprise. "My God Ned, what happened to you?" Erma climbed down from the ladder and stood behind the counter holding her hand to her mouth.

"Yeah, you look good too." Ned replied. "Had a bit of an accident out on the line."

Samuel and Joseph gently seated Ned on a wooden bench set just below the boot shelf where a customer might try on different pairs and sizes. Ned winced as his pants met the wooden slats. The injured man had spent the last two and one half days bouncing and bumping atop the horse drawn travois sling, it had been a taxing journey despite the birch bark brew than Joseph provided at every meal and before bedding down for the night upon the hard ground.

Ned turned to Samuel and Joseph and smiled weakly. "Mîkwec... thanks fellows, and may God bless you all for getting me back here. Many thanks: Mîkwec." The elder shot Ned a toothless smile, while on the trail, Joseph attempted to teach Ned some of the Cree languages more common words. Motioning for his son Jimmy to attend him, Samuel left the store for several minutes leaving the old man sitting on the bench alongside Ned.

Erma couldn't hold back the question any longer. "Mr. Appleton." She paused, watching Ned and Schofield turn their attention toward her. "Mr. Appleton. What of George Dunn! Is he all right?"

It took a moment for Ned to place the girl. He smiled quickly replying. "Yes my dear. He's just fine." He watched the tension and concern on Erma's face fade into a mixture of relief and gratitude.

"Did he come home with you?" Erma walked to the windowed storefront looking this way and that into the muddy street.

"No." Ned replied. "Sorry no. He's staying out there for maybe three weeks or so." Samuel and Jimmy came through the door each carrying a large bundle of pelts that they dropped and spread out atop the general store's broad countertop. "As you can see, the season's been good, and George wants to stay on a bit longer." He could see the disappointment in Erma's face and frowned, suddenly realizing she'd have to tell her sister George was still out in the wilderness, on his own and wouldn't be back for nearly a month.

Schofield poured Ned a mug of hot coffee. Ned took a sip then pointed to the larger bundle of pelts upon the counter top. He looked to Samuel, "Those are yours, grateful for your troubles and your help." Samuel shook his head declining the offer, but Ned would have none of it. "Samuel, Jimmy, Joseph. Without you I might well not be sitting here today!" The men exchanged a round of farewells then the three Cree departed the store with a final wave. A moment later, Harry Hyde stood in the doorway looking out into the roadway as Samuel and the others mounted their ponies and rode off down the street.

Ned sat back and sipped his coffee while telling Harry, James, and Erma about his and George's adventures as well as his own mishap. Erma sat on a stool listening carefully to the entire conversation, knowing she'd have to repeat it verbatim once she got back to the cabin. To his credit, Ned said nothing of George's encounter with the wolverine until Erma had left for home.

Resurrection

The following morning, George had retrieved the wolverine's body from the trap. Examining the hide, he found several of the stakes had penetrated its chest and abdomen; still George felt it was worth skinning out, even if only to be tacked upon his cabin wall for posterity. There was little question the story behind the hide would be an ideal conversation starter. He added the pelt with the rest, but only after allowing it to soak in the river overnight then wrap it tightly within freshly cut fir boughs in an attempt to dispel its musky stench.

As planned, George didn't bother going to the trouble of establishing a permanent camp, opting instead to erect a simple shelter at the end of each day as he moved about discovering the best opportunities and locations for his traps and snares. So far, although late in the season, George became optimistic his new line would out produce the old, and in a shorter space of time. As he tended the campfire he'd built on the third day of his trek, he thought it ironic that the marauding wolverine would wind up being responsible for what he anticipated would be a resounding success. Tomorrow morning he'd set out and begin visiting the traps and deadfalls he'd set the first day after dispatching the wolverine.

The next morning he reached the first of the steel traps he'd set near a small beaver pond. As he approached the trap's location, he could see a furry body floating atop the water bordering the shoreline. The ice nearest the surrounding shoreline was always the first to melt and while doing so had created an island of snow and ice floating in the middle of the pond. The ice island began about ten feet from the shore on all sides, an unbroken outer ring of shallow open water.

George had carefully positioned the trap along a narrow log in such a way that should a beaver or muskrat be caught by the leg, it would struggle against the trap and in the process either jump or fall into the water. The weight of the trap and chain would soon exhaust the animal and being unable to regain its footing on the log the luckless animal would quickly drown. The idea lying behind this particular setup was easy though cruel; an animal couldn't gnaw off its own leg and escape the trap if it were dead.

George picked up a nearby stick. Hooking and tugging the metal chain anchoring the trap he dragged the trap and body toward shore. The lack of resistance to his efforts immediately told him something was amiss. Having laid the body of the beaver ashore, the reason quickly became apparent. Half the body was missing, torn away and eaten. Knowing that both black and grizzly bears considered beaver a delicacy, he tramped about the shoreline looking for any sign or indication of their track, but found none. Not that he expected to, this high up most bears would still be in hibernation, besides, they wouldn't leave so much as a morsel remaining. Maybe an eagle had dined on the beaver; either way George figured it would remain a mystery. He reset the trap before moving on to inspect the others he'd set along the pond's shoreline. Untriggered, the others still lay as he'd set them days before. When he'd ventured further along his trap line, he discovered everything was in order and happily took a fine bounty of pelts. It seemed that he'd dealt with the threat to his livelihood. With any luck, he'd head for home in a week or two at most and the furs he brought with him would fetch enough money to see him and Grace through until fall's harvest.

Iska had lost more than two days trying to ford the river, yet remained relentless in her pursuit. Now only moments earlier, she had discovered the man's faint scent leading from the river's southern shore and into the forest. She discovered his trail difficult to follow. The scent wasn't windborne and whatever scant odor she could detect lay hidden within an infrequent boot print in the snow bare ground. The track led along a long series of the washboard like, tree-lined hummocks. These small mounds and larger hills fanned eastward in ever diminishing ripples until finally disappearing upon meeting the Great Plains. Toward the north and south, these foothills lay bordered to the west by the majestic peaks of the snow-capped Rockies. Against these challenges, the angeline displayed incredible patience and fortitude. Now unless something more urgent drew her attention, she'd press onward until either the enemy had fled her territory, or she destroyed him.

It was late evening on the third day when she picked up the markings and spoor of a male wolverine intruding on the southern boundary of her range. She had a decision to make. Should a larger and more powerful wolverine appear would she defend her range from the challenger? If a confrontation took place and she was the inferior animal, Iska risked losing part or all of her range to the intruder. The deciding factor was George's continuous trespass within her territory; her nature wouldn't allow her to surrender the hunting ground uncontested to either the man or another wolverine. For now, she'd follow the track of the male wolverine, safely surveilling him from distance, there was always the chance she may discover he was a juvenile and yield the territory unfought. Should he prove too formidable, she'd retreat within her range leaving the troublesome human to become the male wolverine's problem.

INTUITION RUNS AMOK

Erma awoke abruptly. Her sister was thrashing in a tangle of sheets and bed covers, moaning in a frightened eerie manner, while experiencing a horrifying and vivid nightmare. Erma had witnessed Grace's recent nocturnal disturbances; they'd become more frequent since Ned's return to the Creek, but tonight's performance was something altogether different.

Erma lit the candle on the night table then turned and evaluated her sister in its light. Grace was sweating profusely, her head twisting atop her pillow while her lips silently moved as if she were trying to say something. Erma moved a hand toward her shoulder. In previous nights, just a light touch calmed her sister, dispelling the underlying worries concerning her absent husband, her wellbeing, and that of her unborn child due in little more than a month or so.

Whatever haunted her dreams tonight refused banishment by any mere touch. As Erma's fingertips fell upon her sister's nightgown, Grace bolted off the mattress, sat upright, eyes wide open and a deafening one-word wailing scream on her lips; "George!"

Fifteen minutes had passed since Grace awoke from a night terror so vivid and realistic that even now she swore to Erma what she'd experienced was more a vision than simply a fading dream. Grace described a series of chilling events with incredible detail while seated at the cabin's small table. The wood stove's black fire box glowed a dull red hue in the heat of the fire; a faint pleasant aroma of wood smoke and the candle's burning paraffin drifted within the cabin blunting the sharp edge of Grace's trepidation.

"George was being followed by some evil blood thirsty creature. I could see everything through the beast's eyes, almost as if I were the animal. I saw its nose pressed close to the ground sniffing a footprint and picking up George's trail. Its glowing eyes somehow saw everything clearly, even in the pitch black of night! Its footsteps were silent; it almost floated like a ghost across the ground." Grace's hands shook as she grasped the metal mug of hot tea grateful to warm her chilled fingertips.

Erma sat across the table from her sister wearing a worried expression. As Grace spoke, Erma weighed her sister's condition given the intensity of emotion displayed within the woman's voice and upon her face. This type of thing wasn't at all good for the child; even now, Erma could see the outline of a tiny arm or leg moving below the nightgown stretched across her sister's swollen belly. Erma's mother and aunts often spoke of expectant mothers who having experienced intense surprise or emotion, good or bad, found themselves driven into an early and untimely delivery. In the 1880s, a premature birth was likely a death sentence to the child and possibly a disastrous complication to its mother.

Grace broke through Erma's thoughts as she continued to relate her vision. "Suddenly I was standing beside George as he knelt below a large tree. I looked up and saw a black shape sitting on a tree branch above us. The thing was looking down at George, it looked like..." Grace struggled for the words. "... Like a demon, with its sharp fangs, long claws, and glowing blood red eyes! I tried to warn George, I opened my mouth, but I couldn't speak, scream, or even utter a sound. There he was, my husband, kneeling with his head down and working with his hands, completely oblivious to the danger overhead...." Grace looked off toward the stove. "A moment later it sprang down on top of him..." Grace stopped mid-sentence turning a mute, panic-stricken face toward her sister.

After several tense moments, Erma just had to ask. "And?" Grace stared at Erma wearing a blank expression. "And... Grace!" She raised her voice. "Grace, then what happened?"

"And then you woke me up! You silly thing..." The girls looked at each other for a long moment, before Grace began to giggle nervously. Erma's concerned face lightened within a small grin that widened as she began to laugh along with her sister.

"My God, I'm being ridiculous aren't I sister?" Grace's smile faded as she wondered about herself.

Erma's voice tightened as she extended her hand across the table toward her sister. "No Grace, being worried about your husband is hardly ridiculous." As her palm lay gently upon her sister's clasped hands and interlaced fingers, Erma stated. "Say, why don't we drop into town and ask about. Maybe someone has news?"

"Yes. Yes, that's what we'll do! We need more flour anyway." Almost at once, Grace's worries seemed to fly from her face and vanish into the night. "What do you say we try to get back to sleep after our tea? I promise not to hog all the covers..."

A Trap Walk

It had been a little more than a week since George had caught and killed the male wolverine in the box trap. That morning George knocked down his lean to, loaded his sled, and began his final round along what the Elder Joseph had referred to as the trap walk. The night before, he'd considered his options, finally settling on a plan that would see him return home after collecting any pelts, packing up his traps, and springing any remaining snares or deadfalls. George had few choices left to him. The season was quickly ending and his supplies were nearly exhausted, even considering having received Ned's additional portion of their provisions. The wolverine's attack on the trailhead camp had made short work of those.

The first round he'd made along the trap line had proved more successful than he could have dreamt. Aside from the partially eaten beaver in the pond, none of the other traps had been unusually disturbed; in fact, he'd taken nearly as many pelts on this new trap walk as he had during three rounds about the old line. Together with the hides he managed to salvage from Iska's attack on the trailhead camp, George estimated that upon completion of this final round, he'd have a weeklong journey back to Pincher Creek and into Grace's arms.

Finally, the last day on the line arrived. George had been away from home for nearly four months, it seemed like an eternity. Aside from muttering to himself, George hadn't spoken to or seen another person in well over three weeks, not since Ned left the trailhead with Samuel and the others. Even now while preparing to leave the high country behind, he found himself terribly homesick and preoccupied. His mind wandered thinking about his reunion with Grace, had she had their child? No, not yet he told himself trying to put away any worry of her pregnancy and instead focusing as to how they'd sit about the cabin table drinking coffee, planning the spring planting and catching up on all the happenings in the Creek over the winter.

George promised himself that after the baby came, he'd take Grace into Schofield's and buy her a new dress, maybe even a new bonnet. Now nearly ready for the journey home, the total number of pelts, while still somewhat fewer in number than he'd hoped, were still more than adequate to assure he and Grace would have the money they needed.

Iska heard George's approach well before the man came into view. She quickly climbed fifteen feet up into a large fir and hid behind its sizable trunk. Now motionless, only her head was visible, her eyes peering out through a patchwork of deep green fir boughs.

Only the night before, she'd been following the track of the male wolverine. It was just after sunrise when she came across George's box trap. The man's repugnant smell was everywhere, as was the scent of the male wolverine she'd been following. Extraordinarily cautious at this point, it took her well over an hour of reconnoitering before Iska could bring herself to visit the trap. George had dismantled one side of the box trap to expose the body of the impaled wolverine. Iska smelled the blood on both the sharpened stakes and surrounding ground before she followed the strongly scented trail George had laid when dragging the body of the dead wolverine back to his camp.

Reaching the now empty campsite, she nosed around the area. A short distance off in the woods she found the discarded, denuded body of her "would be" challenger. Not that he would have been much of a challenge; he'd been young, immature, and inexperienced, probably only leaving his mother the previous autumn, as such, he wouldn't have yet reached an acceptable breeding age.

Only taking the occasional mouse or vole she'd happened across; Iska hadn't had a decent meal in several days. Dining on the young male's corpse, she ate her fill before deciding to sleep and leave her search for the human intruder after nightfall. In the meantime, she'd continue exploring the nearby area. Her sensitive nose quickly led her to the deadfall George had set below a large tree. The body of a marten lay half-covered by a heavy rock, killed when it disturbed the bait triggering the deadfall.

Iska prepared to rob the trap, but paused hearing something moving down the trail in her direction. Her radar like ears identified the rhythmic footfalls as belonging to the trespassing human. She immediately abandoned the idea of robbing the trap and suddenly feeling frightened and alarmed originally considered flight, but too far from the safety of dense brush, she chose instead to climb. Gaining height, she gained bravery.

Perhaps seeing George walking into view only some hundred yards distant was an amazing stroke of luck. Maybe she'd find out what the human tasted like as well.

Any News?

Pulling their wagon up to Schofield's storefront, Grace and Erma stepped down securing Old Red to the hitching post, and then climbed onto the porch. Pausing a moment before entering the establishment, the women noticed Harry Hyde standing behind the counter, a rifle lying on the countertop between the proprietor and Ed Southern, a well-known local rancher. Ed picked the rifle up from the countertop inspecting the open breech before looking down its barrel and checking its iron sights.

Grace and Erma stepped inside. Harry, upon hearing the tinkle of the little bell mounted above the doorway, nodded a quick greeting toward the women while Ed Southern turned about. "Grace, Erma, nice to see you." Ed smiled.

"Nice to see you as well Mr. Southern, tell us now, how is Francine? Has she recovered from the flu?" Grace asked.

Ed replied. "She's fine, thanks for asking."

"You be sure to say that we asked after her now." Like George and every other man Grace had ever known, Ed probably wouldn't mention her inquiry; heck, as a group they wouldn't even bother mentioning they met the Queen of England.

The men turned their attention back to the Martini-Henry rifle Ed held in his hands leaving Grace and Erma to set about and pick up a few essentials.

Harry carried on with his sales pitch. "This very model is one and the same as that used by the British Army when it fought the Zulu nation some ten years back." Nearly everyone living anywhere in the British Empire had heard of the Zulu wars, the event having been reported and widely published by the world's major papers. The Battle of Rorke's Drift in January of 1879 was touted a glorious victory. During the battle, a small force of British soldiers bravely defeated a much larger band of hostile warriors. Many of her majesty's gallant defenders received the Victoria Cross, the largest number ever awarded during a single encounter.

"That so..." Ed rubbed his hand across the long gun's polished buttstock.

Martini-Enfield Mk I Rifle

Looking over to Grace who had just placed a small can of pepper atop beside some other goods she and Erma had already stacked off to one side of the countertop, Harry's face lit up. "Matter of fact, Grace's husband George bought one just like it last summer. Isn't that so Grace?"

Ed didn't appear overly impressed while he worked the gun's action. "My wife has a cousin living on a farm just outside Pretoria; he's one of those Boers, goes by the name of van der Walt, or something like that. He wrote Francine sayin' the newspapers down there mentioned another battle some weeks before... turns out the Brits lost an entire command of thirteen hundred men. They had this very same gun too." Harry's head spun toward Ed, his face wearing a deep frown. Noticing Harry's disapproving expression, Ed reddened slightly as he suddenly remembered George's absence and Ned's premature return from the high country. "My apologies Grace." He quickly followed up. "I'm sure George is just fine."

Grace's face had fallen, but she managed a quiet reply. "Thank you Mr. Southern, I'm sure he'll return safely to us all soon." Erma simply glared at both men.

The tension was suddenly relieved when James Schofield walked in from the storeroom and addressed the girls in a cheerful voice. "Grace, Erma. How are you two ladies faring today, Harry getting everything you need?" The group chitchatted for several minutes until Grace bridged the question that had been nagging at her since her last visit to town.

"Mr. Schofield... James. You haven't by any chance heard any news of George?" Grace's voice had a tinge of desperation that wasn't lost on anyone within the room.

"I'm sorry Grace. We haven't heard any news at all." Jim shook his head.

Harry piped up trying to sound a little more upbeat. "Will say this, a few provisioners down from the Kootenays and on their way back to Fort McLeod say the trapping season's been so good that some fella's have been staying out a might longer than usual." He voice lowered a bit before offering quietly. "Maybe George has chosen to do the same."

A man cleared his throat behind the small group. Every head turned. A stocky man wearing the uniform of the Northwest Mounted Police stood in the doorway; a pair of chevrons sewn onto the shoulders of his tunic. "Excuse me all, but I couldn't help overhearing." Unknown to any in the group, the sergeant, in the company of a young recruit had only arrived minutes before; the young officer was presently at the livery having his horse reshod. The senior officer continued and speaking in a deep baritone voice introduced himself. "Sergeant Wilt Brownly."

After the introduction, the sergeant went on to say that he and his constable were on a patrol that would take them as far west as the Kutanie Pass cross roads. That is where they were to meet three additional recruits riding down from Calgary and guide them to their new posting at Fort MacLeod. When the recruit's horse threw a shoe just outside of town, the sergeant figured they'd visit the blacksmith then pick up a few more supplies before moving west and onto the cross roads.

Fifteen minutes later, the young officer arrived at the store. Sergeant Brownly was just finishing his second cup of coffee and assuring Grace they'd be sure to stop into the store and share any news of her husband.

Riding atop the buckboard on their way home, Grace wondered if she really wanted to know whatever news might arrive, or that if ignorance, however temporary, was truly bliss... at least given such an unforeseeable outcome. By the time the women arrived at the farm, Grace had decided to leave it to God and whatever the fates might have in store. Either way, she would face the future directly and steadfast. Still, one thing was quickly growing clear; if George didn't arrive within several weeks time, he'd be meeting both her and his new child.

OF LIFE AND DEATH

Iska remained hidden within the fir boughs as silent and as still as death. Although she had many questions regarding the strange human creature, she'd come to respect the fact that it had somehow managed to dispatch one of her own kind. Yet so far she'd discovered humans seemingly possessed little if no sense at all of smell, couldn't see or at least didn't chance moving after dark, but yet somehow, it possessed control over her arch nemesis; fire. Now, watching the man's careless approach, she felt she'd already gained the upper hand, and at least for now, she'd rely on stealth as her greatest weapon.

Whether prey or predator, an animal not yet having experienced contact with a human will not possess an innate fear of man, the fear of humanity is a learned response, passed on by an adult to its young, or a lesson learned on an individual basis. In this case, caution was an instinctive response, keeping a safe distance was always prudent until learning more of the adversary. In the past, Iska had faced down truly dangerous animals when driving them off their kills be they wolves, bears or even cougar. While she preferred discovering or stealing carrion, when the rare opportunity presented itself, she also dispatched deer and young elk; prey both larger and fleeter of foot than she. On those times, like today, she had hidden herself within trees waiting to ambush the prey should they move beneath her position. When she felt the time was right she'd leap downward onto their backs and slide about the lower portion of the animal's neck locking her powerful jaws on its throat in a death grip that quickly strangled the animal.

Now the trespasser was approaching her location in the same manner, oblivious to her presence and seemingly intent on nothing more than retrieving the body of the marten from beneath the deadfall. George stood directly below her. She waited patiently, peering over the branch and watching the man stoop, lift the rock and remove the martin's body. Iska found herself facing a decision. Should she merely threaten the man, drive it from his kill and off her range, or follow the much more dangerous choice, carry out a predatory attack - ambush and kill the human who strayed below.

It had been a good morning. Nearly half the traps George checked had taken animals, and the last deadfall along his trap line produced a large martin. He'd skin it out, placing the pelt on the sled with the others before starting his trek homeward. Removing the limp body of the marten, he laid it upon the flat killing rock. In practiced error, he removed his long hunting knife rather than the short curved blade always used for skinning. This small mistake would save his life.

George was about to replace the long knife within its belt sheath, when he suddenly felt a weight strike his back like a sledgehammer. A quick panic immediately set in temporarily causing him to freeze while his mind tried to evaluate the situation. Whatever had attacked him had rolled off his back, at least for the moment. A near blinding pain informed him that sharp claws had raked his back and right side, thank God the cold weather had forced him to bundle up, otherwise those claws might well have torn him wide open.

Iska felt the moment had arrived; she sprang down upon the human from a height of nearly ten feet. Striking the human's back, her powerful front and back claws dug and easily penetrated the creature's hide, but unlike any other animal she'd ever attacked in a similar way, the claws refused to grip and hold her atop the prey. Instead, the strange skin tore and rolled loosely about the animal's bulk. Prevented from establishing a solid purchase, her body slid to one side while momentum took over throwing Iska violently to the earth. She rolled over several times finding her feet and righting herself, but the confidence of a quick kill eluded her, and she paused for several long moments. In those few seconds, Iska watched the man spin about and face her while on his knees. How curious the angeline thought; it didn't bar its teeth, raise its claws in warning or even try to flee. Her confidence now completely re-established she began what she felt would be her final and successful charge.

Whatever the animal was, it had grabbed hold of his coat and clung tight spinning George to the right and briefly onto his back. Assisted by the flow of adrenaline, he rolled onto his stomach using his hands to brace himself against the frozen earth. In a flash, he rose to his knees to face his attacker. Seeing Iska before him, George was incredulous, he'd fully expected a cougar as he'd seen the animal's track and spoor from time to time, but he'd never thought to face the bared fangs of a wolverine that snarled and menaced only several yards distant. Somehow, the surprise of the attack had caused George to hold his knife within a death grip. Unable to chance rising to his feet, George continued to kneel awaiting the attack that would no doubt follow. Glancing downward, he was surprised and grateful to find the long razor sharp blade still held out before him.

Iska covered the distance between her and George in what seemed to both to be less than a second. The creature carried the reek of death itself, the rotting carrion between her fangs and her pungent musky odor spearheading her attack. Tooth and fang, Iska snarled springing toward the man's throat, her long front claws extended outward and before her to either side of her jaws. Her plan of attack was both simple and effective. Grasping the prey with her powerful claws and holding it close, her fangs would rip the life from its body.

George instinctively turned his face raising his left arm to intercept the wolverines gaping jaws and protect his throat although in that same instant the hooked claws along her right foot met his forehead and raked downward, gouging deep furrows in his scalp, and narrowly missing his right eye while leaving his cheek a ragged bloody ruin.

Yet it wasn't to fall in the wolverines favor.

As Iska leapt in midair, George's right hand swept the knife upward; the point of the blade penetrating her body just below the chest before continuing to slice upward. Ironically, her acrobatic leap served only to guide the blade's action. Moving within her chest, its razor edge severed her upper liver, cut through her lungs before finally piercing her heart.

George felt the knife ripped out of his hand, the powerful claws of a rear foot tearing at its bone handle, but only after the knife had cut deeply within her body. Knowing himself now defenceless, George curled up in a ball upon the earth. His bloody hands reached about his head and neck hoping to protect his vitals from the animal's vicious attack while he waited for its final charge. The end of her assault would come suddenly and unexpectedly.

George's knife had done its work. The wolverine was already dead, but to Iska these egregious wounds were presently little more than a distraction. Ignoring her pain, Iska's iron will remained fixed upon George's utter destruction. In the last five seconds of her life, her compact muscular body would drive tooth and claw in a relentless attack ending only when blood loss and lack of oxygen eventually rendered her unconscious.

The forest fell into absolute silence. George lay on the ground, still tightly curled into a ball. Why had the beast not followed up its attack? What was it waiting for - it so clearly had won the battle. After nearly thirty seconds or so, he chanced a movement and stuck out his uninjured arm from beneath his body.

Nothing happened.

He waved his arm about. He was trying to attract the beast's attention while praying not to succeed.

Once again, nothing?

He heard a raven's harsh voice croak out to its mate. Moments afterward, he heard the bird's approach. Its large wings flapped leisurely overhead before fading into the distance. George raised himself to one knee cautiously surveying the scene. The wolverine lay five feet away, unmoving, its jaws open and bloody, its eyes held within a death stare, affixed upon some distant unseen vista.

Struggling to his feet, George staggered over to his sled sitting down on the oilskin covering the mound containing his equipment and pelts. It took him several minutes to realize the immediate danger had passed and several more to understand that a less urgent, but a no less lethal peril remained.

The fingers of his uninjured arm traced a deep gouge running across his forehead. Wiping away the blood that spilled into his eyes, George thought it didn't hurt as badly as it should have. Dropping the hand to his cheek revealed a different story entirely. His torn cheek erupted in a bright painful vengeance. George quickly withdrew the hand as his tongue explored the inside of the injured cheek. Pressing against a particularly painful area, he felt the tip of his tongue breach the flesh and poke outward into the ice-cold air. Glancing downward towards the chest of his jacket, he could see he'd lost a considerable amount of blood. He had to act fast. Rummaging through his clothing, he came across a grey, previously snow white scarf, and bound his ruined face as tightly as the pain would allow.

Minutes afterward, George examined the exterior of his torn coat and removing it, saw the tattered sweater and plaid shirt below. The material was soaked bloody and clung above the thin and hopefully shallow furrows marking his right side and stomach. Noting the blood had already begun to clot, George decided against disturbing the cloth and possibly causing renewed bleeding and blood loss.

Feeling sick to his stomach, light headed and extremely thirsty, George recognized the signs of shock. He quickly built a good sized fire a yard or so from his sled, drank his canteen nearly dry before forcing his way through the pain in his mouth downing a can of beans and salt pork. A few minutes later, he vomited, bringing at least half of the meal back up. Although weak and dizzy, he slowly gathered firewood laying it within arm's reach then spread his bedroll atop the ground beside the sled. Covering himself with a combination of blankets and clothing he figured that with luck, he'd manage to keep himself warm and alive throughout the remainder of the day, but there was some doubt as to how he would fare during the long night.

The following day had dawned cold and bright and judging from the sun's position, George figured he'd slept until mid-morning. The firewood had run out shortly before dawn, but the early spring sun helped warm his body. He stood up shakily while taking stock of his condition. Much of his strength had returned although his cheek continued to bleed every time he moved his jaw or made the mistake of running his tongue across the wound.

George was pleased to discover the wounds on his side and belly were mostly superficial, though occasionally excruciating. He'd dug inside a soiled cloth bag and as a gifted songwriter would scribble down in the future, "located his cleanest dirty shirt." He slowly pried the blood-dried shirt from his side with an agonizing slowness, trying his best not to reopen the wound any more than was necessary before cleaning and redressing the wound.

Fifteen minutes later, the leather sled harness lay draped across his shoulders awaiting the first tug of many on his way home. His eyes fell upon the wolverine. He set the harness aside, took out his skinning knife, and dressed the animal making sure to keep the head still attached to the pelt; this would be a souvenir. He took a deep breath before starting out down the trail for home. He just hoped the wounds wouldn't fester, other than the possibility of infection, George felt confident he could make it.

Almost Home

Erma had been working in the store when a young Northwest Mounted police constable she'd never seen before ran through Schofield's doorway. The small bell above the door was still swaying and tinkling when he spoke rather breathlessly. "There a doctor in this town?"

Erma ran into the back room and moments later brought Harry Hyde and James Schofield running into the store.

"There a doctor in town?" The constable again shouted out, appearing somewhat frustrated.

Harry replied. "Hold on there young fellow. Yes, we have a doctor, at least of sorts." Bill Whipple's as close as we come. Fellow owns the livery cross the way. Trained as a vet, but happens to do a little human doctoring on the side. Want a real doctor; you have to go all the way into Fort Macleod."

James Schofield held up a palm. "Now settle down for a second. Just what on earth happened and who did it happen to?" he asked.

"My Sergeants on his way with the rest of our patrol and an injured trapper... we found him and his sled lying beside a pile of rocks at the western crossroads. There he was, wrapped in an oilskin atop a bedroll laid out beside a sled full of pelts. Sergeant says he figures the fellow's got the fever. The man's talking some nonsense about fightin' some demon or other." The young man licked his lips nervously.

"This trapper have a name son?" asked Harry.

"Yes sir. Goes by the name of Dunn... George Dunn." The constable replied. "Can we hurry it up with the doc; my sergeant will be here pretty soon, they aren't far behind me."

Harry turned to Erma. "Girl! Get yourself out to the farm and fetch your sister here as quick as you can."

Hyde didn't have to ask twice, she'd already gotten her coat and was running out the door. James Schofield followed her out; "I'll fetch Bill!"

Harvest

The night was comfortably warm for mid-October, and a huge orange moon had cleared the horizon bathing the thatched stacks of wheat and barley sheaves lying in neat rows in soft light and shadow. The next day would see the sheaves picked and loaded into Dunn's wagon. The season had provided an excellent harvest. Schofield reported the prices for grain were up in Fort Macleod and all points east. The farmers in the area would do well.

A couple sat in two of four wooden chairs set atop the cabin's new porch George built that summer. A young woman sipped from her mug of hot tea while a man helped himself to a second biscuit the woman had baked fresh earlier that afternoon.

Smiling appreciably Ned Appleton said, "You're a fine baker Erma." Since Ned's return, he and Erma had been seeing a lot of each other. People were already wondering when they'd tie the knot.

Moments later, the cabin door creaked opened and Grace walked through the doorway and onto the porch, a sleeping babe in her arms. Following his wife, George paused in the doorway, turning slightly his eyes strayed across the back cabin wall where they came to rest upon an oval board hung in the center of the log wall. A patch of thick fur lay stretched across the board's thin wicker frame. Within its center was an island of grizzled dark brown fur set in a sea of a gold blonde mane drifting out toward its sides. A flowing dark tail drooped below the pelt while along a side hung a bleached sharp-jawed skull.

Recollecting his struggle with the wolverine, George placed his palm on his face, his finger tracing the long scarred furrow running down his cheek and exploring whatever patches of beard survived Iska's mauling. He'd never see her like again. He'd also foresworn never to venture anywhere near the mountain range to which she or any of her kind might lay claim.

Turning away, George stepped onto to the front porch looking towards his wife and child. His life was in the lowlands, a simple farmer raising his family on the vast golden prairie. A man thankful he'd one day relate his encounter with the legendary Kwekwatshew to his new son.

Manufactured by Amazon.ca
Bolton, ON

34895120R00072